An Amish Christmas

**Center Point
Large Print**

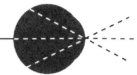

**This Large Print Book carries the
Seal of Approval of N.A.V.H.**

An Amish
Christmas

Cynthia Keller

CENTER POINT LARGE PRINT
THORNDIKE, MAINE

This Center Point Large Print edition is
published in the year 2010 by arrangement with
Ballantine Books, an imprint of
The Random House Publishing Group,
a division of Random House, Inc.

Copyright © 2010 by Cynthia Keller

An Amish Christmas is a work of fiction.
Names, characters, places, and incidents are the
products of the author's imagination or are used
fictitiously. Any resemblance to actual events, locales,
or persons, living or dead, is entirely coincidental.

The text of this Large Print edition is unabridged.
In other aspects, this book may vary
from the original edition.
Printed in the United States of America.
Set in 16-point Times New Roman type.

ISBN: 978-1-60285-954-8

Library of Congress Cataloging-in-Publication Data

Keller, Cynthia.
An Amish christmas / Cynthia Keller.
   p. cm.
ISBN 978-1-60285-954-8 (library binding : alk. paper)
1. Amish—Fiction. 2. Christmas stories. 3. Large type books. I. Title.
PS3572.I263A83 2010b
813'.54—dc22

                                                    2010029736

To Mark, Jenna,
and Carly

for whom I am grateful each and every day

And
for Jean Katz

we battle the darkness of sorrow
with the brilliant light of loving memory

Acknowledgments

It is a lucky writer who has the good fortune to have colleagues who are also friends. I have known and collaborated on many projects with my agent, Victoria Skurnick, for over two decades. She is supremely generous in deed and spirit, fantastically smart, and the most kindhearted person I know. She can also make me laugh until I cry, one of my favorite qualities in a person. In good times, she is the first to applaud me, and in bad, the first to extend a helping hand. It is a true privilege to call her my friend.

A special thank-you goes to Sharon Fantera, who is the godmother of this book and without whom it would not exist.

My editor, Linda Marrow, has been fantastic in every way, from her early support to her encouragement and wise suggestions. She is all you could want in an editor—plus, we had fun. I am thrilled and grateful that I had this opportunity to work with her.

I hope my husband and children know how touched I have been by their tireless cheerleading and their desire to help in whatever way I asked. Sharing this experience with you three has made it that much more meaningful. I love you with all my heart.

An Amish Christmas

Chapter 1

"You're looking a little pathetic there, Mom."

As her daughter, Lizzie, entered the kitchen, the words startled Meg from her reverie. Leaning on both elbows at the kitchen's butcher-block island, she'd been staring, unseeing, at the large tray of untouched cookies before her. She reached up to remove the tall witch's hat she'd been wearing for the past two hours, and set it down beside the tray.

"They're such cute cookies, aren't they?" Meg asked her daughter in a wistful voice. "Not one trick-or-treater this year. I can't believe it."

Lizzie, her laptop computer tucked under one arm, paused to stare at her mother's handiwork. "*Dude,* how long did it take you to make all these? They're insane."

"Don't call me 'dude,' " Meg responded automatically. "I thought it would be fun to try something different. It wasn't a big deal."

She had no intention of confessing to her fifteen-year-old how long the process had taken. After finally locating the correct chocolate cookies—the ones with the hollow centers—she had used icing to "glue" chocolate Kisses, points up, into the middles, then she'd painstakingly drawn hatbands and bows with a tiny tube of red icing. The result was rows and rows of miniature witch hats. Adorable. They would end up being tossed into the bottomless pits that were the stomachs of her thirteen-year-old son, Will, and his friends.

"Honestly, why do you bother?" Lizzie's muffled voice came from inside their walk-in pantry closet. Meg knew her daughter was grabbing her favorite evening snack, two Pop-Tarts that she would eat right out of the foil package. "No one cares. It's stupid."

Meg quietly sighed. Maybe it *was* stupid to hang the tissue ghosts from the trees in their front yard. To carve the jack-o'-lantern that was the centerpiece of the arrangement on the front steps, with hay, gourds, stuffed scarecrow, and all. Okay, so Lizzie and Will were too old for the giant figures of witches and goblins that she'd taped on the windows. Lizzie was at some in-between stage, too cool to trick-or-treat but probably looking forward to next year, when some of the kids would have driver's licenses. Meg anticipated there would be parties at different houses, no doubt with alcohol involved; she wasn't looking forward to that phase. Will had also declined going from house to house this year, preferring to goof around with his buddies on someone's driveway basketball court. But she'd thought Sam, her nine-year-old, might still have gotten a kick out of her decorations. Wrong. He never appeared to notice them, and he'd barely made it through a half hour of ringing doorbells before declaring he'd had enough of this holiday. What on earth had happened to Halloween being so much crazy fun, the way it was when she was a child? Didn't kids know how to enjoy a holiday anymore? Besides, she *was* cutting back on the fuss; in the past, she would have spent hours baking cookies for trick-or-treaters. This year she had simply combined premade ingredients.

Lizzie, armed with her snack, left the room as the jarring noise of the garage door opening announced that Meg's husband was home. She watched James enter and set down his briefcase in the mudroom before coming toward her. He looked exhausted. As the top in-house legal counsel to a large software corporation, he more than earned his salary. Somehow he managed to withstand endless pressure, maintain constant accessibility, and coolly handle one crisis after another. And those were only a few of his job requirements, it seemed to her.

Pulling off his suit jacket, he gave Meg a perfunctory kiss on the cheek.

"Happy Halloween," Meg said brightly.

"Ummm." His attention was already on the day's mail, which he retrieved from its customary spot on one of the counters. He was frowning as he flipped through the envelopes.

"Something wrong?"

"Too many bills, Meg." He sounded angry. "Too many bills. It's got to stop."

She didn't reply. In eighteen years of marriage, James had rarely complained about their bills. Sure, he wasn't thrilled with paying private school tuition for three children, but it was something he and Meg both wanted to do. Beyond that, it was understood between them and even among their friends that his wife was the saver and he was the spender.

Meg had always understood that *things* were important to her husband. It was he who purchased the designer suits, their fancy watches, her expensive jewelry. It was he who booked the first-class vacations. He was the one, in fact, who chose this enormous house. Even with three children, Meg had no idea why they needed five thousand square feet in one of the most expensive sections of Charlotte.

It was clear that growing up with very little had left a psychological scar on James that he tried to cover up with material trappings. She didn't like it, but she understood. That was what he needed to feel comfortable. He didn't brag or rub his success in anyone's face. Still, it was as if he had to have more of everything just to feel he was level with everyone else.

Recently, though, he seemed to have undergone a change in thinking. He had started complaining regularly about everything she and the children spent

"Are you hungry?" Meg moved to open the refrigerator door.

He slapped the mail back down on the counter. "I mean it! The spending has to stop. We need to batten down the hatches."

She turned back to him. "You're right," she said soothingly. "We will—the hatches, I mean, and the battening. Now, can I get you something to eat?"

"I don't want anything," he snapped. "I'll be in my study."

Meg stared after him. Aside from his sudden financial prudence, he had been uncharacteristically irritable for a while now. And it had been getting worse, she realized, not better. She heard the door to his study slam shut. James was typically calm, even in a crisis. Especially in a crisis, she amended. That was one of the things she loved about him.

They met as sophomores at the University of Illinois in a nineteenth-century American history class. Meg happened to sit next to him one day early in the semester. When he began to juggle a pen, an assignment pad, and an empty soda can, it made her laugh. She grew more interested in him when he was the only one in class who was able to discuss all the major battles of the Civil War before the reading had even been assigned.

Their relationship had started out as more of a friendship. A little teasing back and forth led to some shared coffees, then pizza while studying for the final exam. Slowly, their connection grew and deepened. James proved to be a stabilizing influence on the flighty, directionless girl Meg had been. She had admired his strength, his solidness—not the physical kind but the kind that made her feel cared for and safe. Of course, she reflected with a smile, she hadn't minded that he was tall and broad-chested, with thick sandy-colored hair and large dark eyes whose intent gaze made her feel she was the most important person in the room.

By the end of junior year, it was clear to both of them that marriage would follow on the heels of graduation. While he went to law school, she set up their first apartment and helped support them by working in a boring but well-paying job as an administrative assistant. The plan had always been for Meg to go to law school once James had a job, but then she got pregnant with Lizzie, and that was that. Which was perfectly fine with Meg. She wouldn't trade one minute of time with her three children for anything in the world. Working would have been impractical for her, anyway, since they had moved to three different states over the years because of the series of job offers that came James's way. His drive and early success meant their lives were far more than comfortable. She and the children had everything they could ever need and more.

Maybe too much more.

She heard her older son coming downstairs—his feet, as usual, clomping rapidly rather than just walking. He was talking, his voice growing louder as he approached. "That is so *sick,* man!"

Meg rolled her eyes, understanding this to be high praise for whatever it was Will was discussing. She called out to him.

He stuck his head in the kitchen. He was slender and noticeably tall for an eighth-grader, with a face remarkably like his father's. Will wore a dark-gray sweatshirt, his face nearly hidden in its hood. "Hang on," he said to the room in general. "My mom, yeah."

Meg understood that he was using a hands-free phone. No doubt it was the newest, tiniest, most advanced gadget available. She swore that half the time she didn't know if her children were talking—or listening, for that matter—to her, to one another, or to someone else entirely on a cell phone or computer. Much to her chagrin, her husband aided and abetted the children's desire to be up on the latest electronic everything. It seemed as if he came home every other week with an updated version of some gizmo or other. The stuff just kept changing, rendering the previous purchases obsolete, but no one besides her seemed to mind. Though lately, she reflected, she hadn't seen the usual parade of new electronic toys, so perhaps James had heeded her protests.

"Will, what's the story with the science-fair project?" She tried to keep her tone light. Nonnagging. "And I'd like to see what you're wearing for the class photo tomorrow. No rock-band T-shirts, okay?"

He merely gave her a look as if annoyed by her interruption, then was gone. She heard him resume his conversation in the hall. "Two hundred? So what's the big deal?"

"Well, I certainly straightened *him* out," she muttered. She glanced at her watch. It was past the time she should have started hustling Sam into bed for the night; he invariably dawdled, dragging out the process as long as he could. This evening there had been his minimal trick-or-treating, admiring and organizing the candy he'd collected, and a full load of homework. He still hadn't taken a shower to wash off the remnants of green face makeup from his zombie costume. Rushing now, Meg transferred the cookies to a large plastic container. She frowned as she hurried upstairs; she would have to return to finish cleaning up.

She found her nine-year-old seated at his desk,

pencil in hand, hunched over a math book. He barely had enough space for the book, as his desk was nearly buried beneath the array of papers, random objects, and unidentifiable pieces of who-knew-what. Her younger son collected—anything. Meg didn't know why, but apparently Sam had never met a piece of paper, ticket stub, or souvenir he didn't love. Marbles, miniature cars and action figures, stickers, small plastic animals, and rubbery novelty toys—all were held in equally high esteem. His collection wasn't restricted to his desktop, however, or the desk drawers. Boxes and plastic containers of various sizes were scattered about his room, overflowing with the items Meg periodically gathered up from the floor. She didn't want to think about how many shopping bags full of his stuff were shoved into the back of his closet and on its highest shelves. She was just grateful he restricted himself to smaller treasures. If he'd amassed something like train sets or rocks, they would have been in big trouble.

"Sweetheart," she murmured, her hand on his shoulder. "It's late."

He looked at her and smiled. That grin always melted her heart. While Will looked like James, and Lizzie, with her chestnut-colored hair and hazel eyes, favored Meg, Sam was utterly unlike either one of them. His hair was shiny, almost black, and his brown eyes were so dark that they appeared black as well. Short for his age, with a slight build and pale complexion, he exhibited an inquisitiveness neither of his siblings did.

His nature was different as well. He was far more prone than the other two to feel anxious. He worried and fretted over what might or might not happen in his life, in the country, and in the world. He asked endless questions, which the family called "Sam's what-if questions," about how they would handle a wide range of disasters that might suddenly befall them. Hurricanes, fires, robbers, plagues, waterborne pathogens—Meg was often scrambling to explain how they would escape various calamities. Sam was her sensitive one. Even when the other two were younger, they hadn't seemed quite as fearful. For several years, starting when he was four, Sam often refused to go places that, for some reason or other, sounded frightening to him. It might be another child's birthday party or the beach or the zoo. No amount of reassurance could change his mind.

Thankfully, that phase had passed, but when he got under the covers at night, Meg still spent a few extra minutes sitting on the bed, just hugging him. She knew that, at those times at least, he felt utterly relaxed and safe.

Sam closed his math book and stood. Pale streaks of green makeup were smeared not just on his face but on his arms and T-shirt. There was an outburst of shouting downstairs as Lizzie and Will embarked on what Meg figured had to be their fiftieth argument of the day. Both Sam and Meg ignored the familiar sound.

"Do I have to shower?"

"Yes, sugar, and it has to be fast." Meg smiled as she put her arm around him and led him toward the bathroom.

It was nearly eleven-thirty before all three children were in bed and she had finished cleaning up downstairs. She was exhausted, but, as was her routine, she put on her nightgown and got into bed with her pink leather appointment book—a Mother's Day gift from James two years before—and five pens, each a different color. She had long ago determined that assigning each family member his or her own color made it easier to keep track of who had to be where and when.

She fluffed up two pillows against the headboard and leaned back. She loved this room, with its soothing tones of pale green and beige, the soft cotton sheets and goose-down duvet on the bed, the muted lighting. It was so peaceful here. James still hadn't emerged from his study. Usually, by this hour, he was under the covers, reading a newspaper or business magazine, waiting for her to join him.

She opened her date book, enjoying, as always, the soft leather and thick cream-colored pages. Her own appointments were in red. Tomorrow started with a planning meeting for the high school's spring fund-raiser, after which she had to take in her BMW for a lubc and oil. She made a note to bring her book club's choice for this month to read while she was waiting.

After that, food shopping for the small dinner party they were having on Saturday, so she could start preparing a few days in advance. She would pick up James's dry cleaning and the pearl necklace she was having restrung as a gift for Lizzie, a gift Meg knew would be unwanted now but which she hoped would be appreciated in later years. Then it would be time to drive to piano lessons (a protesting Lizzie—purple ink) and to the shoe store for new sneakers (Sam—blue ink). Swing back around to retrieve Lizzie, then get Will (green ink) from basketball practice at school, and home to make dinner. She scheduled an hour the next night to pay bills and catch up on paperwork.

She turned to her master to-do list, a veritable rainbow of color-coded tasks at the front of the book. Lizzie needed her dental checkup, and Meg jotted that down in purple below the forty-some other tasks on the list. No matter what she did, that list just kept getting longer. It seemed that for every item she completed, another two instantly took its place. Some of the less pressing obligations reappeared month after month, causing Meg guilt pangs over what she viewed as her negligence. Still, there were many days when she wondered what all of this was adding up to. Was there a prize for being the person who accomplished the most errands? Maybe the day you got to the end of your to-do list was the day you died. Just in case, she thought with a smile, *it's a good thing I always leave some stuff undone.*

She closed the book and was placing it on her bedside table when James came into the room. Having left him alone all evening, Meg had assumed that by now his bad mood would have dissipated, but she saw that she was mistaken. His mood was, if anything, darker.

"Honey," she began.

He threw her a hard look. "Not now." He began unbuttoning his shirt, his anger evident in his sharp movements.

"James, what on earth is the matter?" She refused to go along with this any further.

"I said not now," he snapped. Their eyes met, and he softened, his shoulders sagging. "I'm sorry, Meg, I shouldn't . . . I'm really sorry."

She leaned forward. "Why won't you tell me what's going on?"

"Nothing's going on." James exhaled slowly. "It's been a rotten day, that's all. I shouldn't take it out on you."

"You didn't even say hello to the kids tonight. Please tell me what's bothering you."

He sat down on the edge of the bed and kissed her on the lips. "I'm sorry for being a jerk, but I swear, it's nothing." He smiled, shifting gears. "And a very happy Halloween to you, too. Sam better have saved me some of his candy."

"You know our Sam," Meg said lightly, her tone matching his change of mood. "He had a candy bar and some M&M's, then put the rest away to dole out to himself sensibly."

James shook his head. "I can't imagine doing that. My friends and I used to eat ourselves sick on Halloween."

"The simple pleasures of childhood."

He stood. "I'm going to brush my teeth and all that good stuff. Then we'll talk. You'll tell me about your day and the kids' day, and I promise you'll have my undivided attention."

"That's great." Meg smiled at him.

Bending over, he kissed the top of her head, then grinned and went into their bathroom. She heard the water running at his sink, her husband singing an old Bob Dylan song in an exaggerated scratchy voice. It would seem that he had put aside whatever unpleasantness was on his mind. She didn't believe it for a second.

Chapter 2

Meg flipped through a rack of party dresses but made no attempt to pick out anything. She knew that any dress she selected for Lizzie would be met by an immediate veto. Meg understood that she wasn't exactly on top of what teenagers liked to wear, but she didn't think she deserved her daughter's inevitable look of disbelief whenever she held something up for consideration. As far as choosing something for Lizzie to wear to the high school's big Christmas Dance—Meg wasn't even going to try.

She looked over at her daughter, who was searching through racks across the Nordstrom dress department with great intensity. Her mind flashed on Lizzie's early years, when Meg had had the pleasure of outfitting her little girl however she wanted. She remembered the bunny-print pajamas, the white bathing suit with navy-blue bows, a yellow sundress. Little white summer sandals, a tiny jean jacket. That all ended around the time Lizzie turned four, when she insisted that her rainbow T-shirt, flower-print stretch pants, and a white tutu were the perfect outfit for preschool. Every day. And, thought Meg with a smile, when she added the red glitter party shoes, it went so easily from day to evening wear.

"Okay." Lizzie appeared at Meg's side, her arms filled with dresses. "I'm going to try these on."

"Want me to come with you?"

"No." The girl bustled off before her mother could follow.

Meg had spotted a flash of dark purple satin and some black nylon material with big silver sequins among her daughter's choices. She reassured herself that the odds were against Lizzie actually choosing one of those. This was only their first attempt at finding a dress for the dance. No doubt they would have to endure several shopping trips before Lizzie, growing ever more tense and irritable, made the final decision. This was the reason Meg had allocated six weeks to navigate the minefield. All the hysteria had to unfold in, paradoxically, an orderly fashion. If past experience was any indication, Lizzie would question whether she had made the right decision until the moment she walked out the door to attend the actual event.

Sure enough, when Lizzie returned from the dressing room, she was holding only one dress, pale pink with simple beading details and cap sleeves. "What do you think of this one?"

"Very nice," Meg said, reaching for the dangling price tag. She froze. "Five hundred dollars? Are you joking?"

"Oh, Mom, come *on!*" Lizzie snapped. "These kinds of dresses are expensive."

Meg stared at her. "Did I somehow give you the impression that I would spend five hundred dollars on a dress for a school dance? A dress you'll probably wear once?"

"What did you think it would cost? This is what a decent dress goes for. And it looked great on me." Lizzie sounded exasperated. "Excuse me, but what do *your* dresses cost?"

Meg drew herself up. "What my clothes cost is none of your business!"

"Well, how hypocritical is that?"

Meg was infuriated, but at the same time she felt a stab of guilt, knowing that she did have some obscenely expensive clothes hanging in her own closet. James liked her to dress a certain way when they went out. He even seemed to enjoy shopping with her every so often, encouraging her to buy the best suit, the good Italian shoes. Meg also had to admit that she was frequently inconsistent with her daughter, splurging on a ridiculously expensive sweater or skirt for Lizzie, then feeling she had gone too far and sharply drawing the line at another item.

Still, she didn't expect her daughter to take those treats for granted. And she deserved some respect from her child.

"Put the dress back." Her voice was cold. "We're going home."

"What are you talking about? We have to get something."

"No." Meg's eyes flashed. "No, we really don't."

"I can't believe this! All the good dresses will be gone by the time we can go shopping again." Lizzie shook her head. "Come on, Mom. You know you'll want to get me something nice in the end, so there's no point to this."

Meg didn't respond. She strode toward the exit, knowing her daughter had no choice but to follow if she didn't want to walk home. When Lizzie caught up in the parking lot, she was empty-handed and silent. She spent the entire drive home texting on her cell phone. Meg's feelings vacillated between anger at her daughter for her sense of entitlement and annoyance at herself for the way she handled these issues. Sometimes being a parent was so hard, she thought, just so darn hard.

Back at the house, Lizzie slammed the car door and stomped upstairs to her room. Still upset, Meg went to the extra freezer in the garage, peering inside at her choices. She and James were going out that night with two couples, both of the husbands executives in James's department. She had left him a message that morning reminding him. She wasn't looking forward to it, but she understood that socializing was important to his success. Before leaving, she would put something together for the kids' dinner. Lizzie was responsible for watching Sam, something she did periodically and with surprising good nature. Will would be at home as well.

"Lamb chops it is."

Meg reached into the icy air to retrieve the shrink-wrapped package. She dropped the frozen meat into the kitchen sink and set her bag on the counter, hitting the play button on the message machine.

"I tried your cell, but it went right to the message," came her husband's voice. "Did you forget to charge it? I got your message about dinner tonight, but I'd forgotten all about it, and I can't do it anyway. There's an emergency meeting at work, so we have to cancel. I'll take care of it. Don't wait up for me."

An emergency meeting on a Saturday night? If I didn't know better, Meg thought, I'd swear he was cheating on me. Fortunately, she knew he really would be at the office, because things there had been going from bad to worse over the past few weeks. That's where James was right now, spending a sunny Saturday behind his desk.

Of course, he was hardly the only one whose company was in dire economic straits these days. He was closemouthed about the specifics of his firm's troubles, but she could see the stress in his distractedness and growing irritability, not to mention the new dark shadows beneath his eyes.

She had no idea what it all meant, but it frightened her. Was there a chance he might lose his job? He assured her that wouldn't happen, but she read the newspapers and, like everyone else, saw the layoffs going on across the country. In addition, Meg knew virtually nothing about where their savings were invested; James had always handled that end of their finances. She did—and didn't—want to know if they had lost anything substantial in the stock market over the past months. James made it clear he didn't wish to be questioned on these issues, and she knew better than to press him. She had resolved instead to stick her head in the sand because the only other option was to drive herself crazy with pointless speculation. Besides, she thought, it had to be more helpful for everybody if she remained upbeat.

Meg hoped that whatever was going on wouldn't get bad enough to interrupt their Thanksgiving plans. Every year for the five years they had lived in North Carolina, Meg had invited several families in the neighborhood for a huge feast, one she spent a solid week preparing. They were families who, like them, had no other relatives or lived far away from those they did have. Meg always put in a call to her parents, her only living relatives, but they weren't up to making the trip from Homer, New York. Not that they would have come anyway, she knew. Nor, to be honest, would she have wanted them if they did.

Meg had always had a strained relationship with her parents, both of whom were so controlled and controlling, so disapproving of everyone, including her, their only child. She could never understand their narrow-mindedness or why they felt entitled to pass judgment on everyone else's supposed shortcomings. One of the best moments of her life had been finding out she had received a full scholarship to college. The first day of freshman year couldn't come too soon for her. Her parents couldn't understand why she would go to a school so inconveniently far away, and she didn't bother explaining that was exactly why she had chosen it.

Before she was born, her parents had started what grew from a tiny general store to a small department store with a specialty in fishing equipment, selling everything from waders and rods to bait and tackle. They had never forgiven Meg and James for refusing to move back to her hometown and join the family business after they married. Without the couple's participation, the store, their lives' work, would disappear once they could no longer run it.

Their irrational demand had come as an unpleasant shock, and it was pretty much the last straw. Both Meg and James found this long-held grudge incomprehensible. It cast a pall over the few phone conversations she and her parents did have. But Meg tried to remain on decent terms with them for the sake of her children.

She often wished that the three of them had cousins, but James, too, had no siblings. His parents had died in a car accident when he was in his twenties. Sadly, there was no one else, other than James's elderly uncle, who was in a nursing home in California, in the advanced stages of Alzheimer's.

Meg loved Thanksgiving, so, despite the lack of extended family, she went all out. Up went all the construction-paper turkeys and pilgrim hats made by the children over the years in elementary school. She fussed over gourds, cranberries, and Indian corn to create painter-ready still-life arrangements. Berries and bright orange, red, and yellow leaves accented any surfaces that struck her fancy. Meg suspected that, as they had on Halloween, her efforts would go unnoticed at best or, at worst, be ridiculed. Nonetheless, she would do it for herself and for the younger neighborhood children who would be in attendance.

With an unexpected free evening, she could get a head start on her menu plan and to-do list. She went to get some paper, mentally reviewing what needed doing. Just for starters, polish the silver, wash and iron the linens, check the candle supply, bring up the largest serving platters from the basement closet. The list would be a long one. If she was lucky, she might get the kids to help with the platters, but that was about the only work she could expect to wrench out of them.

As she grabbed a pad from the kitchen desk drawer, she glanced up at the bulletin board that held the family's notes and schedules. She saw there was an addition to the Holiday Posting. About a year ago, Will began tacking up a selection of each month's strangest yet real holidays, and it had become a regular feature on the board. Lizzie and Sam also weighed in—all this information culled, Meg supposed, from the Internet, apparently the source for everything in the universe. Or at least their universe. November, it turned out, was Peanut Butter Lovers' Month. Sam had written that it was also Diabetic Eye Disease Awareness Month. Today Meg saw two new contributions in Lizzie's handwriting: Start Your Own Country Day, following right on the heels of Absurdity Day.

Meg laughed. Now, *those* were holidays.

The front door slammed. That would be Will getting dropped off by Michael Connolly's parents.

The two boys often went skateboarding in the park, with Meg and Emma Connolly sharing carpool duty.

Meg heard her son go upstairs. "Hi, honey!"

No response.

She walked out to the bottom of the stairs, spotting Will just before he disappeared from view on the second floor. "Hey, Will, how are you?"

He stopped and took a step back, holding on to his wildly colorful skateboard. "Oh, hi, Mom." He gave her a small smile.

Meg regarded him. Something didn't seem right. For two years, a full set of braces had slightly altered the appearance of his lower face, but in September they had been replaced by a smaller retainer. The facial change was minor, but it was visible to Meg. "Honey, why aren't you wearing your retainer?"

"You're fast, I gotta give you that." He shifted the skateboard in his arms. "Yeah, I was going to tell you."

Uh-oh. This was why he'd tried to bypass her downstairs: so she wouldn't get a good look at him.

"Will?"

"It broke. I left it on a bench, I swear, for, like, two seconds, and somebody must've sat on it or something."

"But the case should have protected it."

Will fiddled with a skateboard wheel.

"Oh. It wasn't in the case." She wrinkled her nose in disgust. "You took your retainer straight from your mouth and put it on a public bench?"

He shrugged. "It was bothering me, so I took it out, and when I came back, it was, like, all bent and busted up."

"Let me take a look. Maybe Dr. Russell can salvage it."

"Trust me, no way."

"Can I at least take a look at it?"

"I threw it out in the park. If you want, we could go get another one in an hour or so. I have some stuff I have to do first."

"Get another one?" Meg's voice rose. "Do you realize that makes three this fall? Three!"

"Mom, it's not my fault! I know I lost the first one, but that could happen to anybody. I can't help it that some jerk broke this one. Besides, that's only two."

"You need a new one. That would make three. At four hundred dollars apiece."

"Oh yeah, I guess you're right. Bummer." He scratched his head distractedly. "So, do you want to go later or what?"

"You can't just drop by the orthodontist's office. Besides, it's Saturday."

"Oh." He moved toward his room. "Okay. Whatever."

Meg gripped the banister in anger. "We invested so much time and money in braces, and now that they're off, you can't be bothered to hang on to a retainer for more than a month. But hey, it doesn't matter, right? We'll just keep replacing them. *Lizzie* has to have a five-hundred-dollar dress! You both *deserve* all these things, naturally. Nobody needs to be grateful or take any responsibility in any way, nobody needs to stop and consider that we are *not*—I know it's hard to believe—*made of money.*"

"Whoa, Mom." Will held up a hand to calm her. "Chill."

"Don't you dare say that to me! You know what? I'm going to leave now before I lose myself. And I'm going to think about why my children are so incredibly spoiled."

There was a pause as Will took this in. "If we're not going to Dr. Russell, can I go over to Dan's house?"

Meg didn't bother to answer. She returned to the kitchen and sat down heavily at the table.

That makes the second time today that my children got me so angry, I literally removed myself from their presence, she thought. Was this normal? Maybe she was too impatient or not understanding enough. They'd always been great kids. Lizzie had been the child with the summer lemonade stand, donating her proceeds to Save the Children, and using her free time to make braided bracelets out of yarn, which she sold to her classmates, again for charity. In middle school, she had been the rare kid who invited every girl in her class to her birthday parties, not wanting anyone to feel left out. Will, too, had a generous side that, just a couple of years ago, led him to organize weekly softball games for the younger kids on their street. Yet lately it was as if some soul-stealing virus had infected them. It left them selfish and utterly full of themselves. Maybe it was just adolescence. But maybe not.

Meg wondered if she should take some action to teach them not to take everything for granted. Maybe she should call off this week's planned visit to the Festival of Lights in Winston-Salem. Every year they took the hayride through Tanglewood Park to marvel at what was reputed to be a million lights arranged in more than a hundred displays. It was an overwhelming sight that signified the start of the Christmas season to them. She sighed. Sam loved going so much; it wasn't fair to punish him because of the older ones.

The phone rang, startling her. She picked it up. "Hello?"

"It's me." James's voice was strained.

"Hi, sweetheart. You okay? Are you really staying at work late tonight?"

"Yes. I just remembered something. The trip in January—you need to cancel it."

Meg tried to hide her disappointment. "Oh. You're sure?"

"Of course I'm sure," he snapped. "I have to go."

She forced a cheerful goodbye and hung up. So much for their romantic getaway to the Cloister in Georgia. The four-day trip was James's anniversary present for her, already postponed once from their actual anniversary in September because of his work. Just the two of them, alone at the most gorgeous, luxurious resort. Ever since the children were little, James had arranged a getaway for the two of them on their anniversary, even if they could manage it for only one night. This was the first time it had ever been put off —and, it occurred to her, he had said to cancel the trip. Not postpone or reschedule. She hoped that was all he was implying, but something told her "cancel" meant exactly what it said.

At any rate, she now had to make a slew of phone calls to deal with the various reservations and people booked for those four days to take care of the children and the house. With a sigh, she located the binder where she kept all her household-related notes and phone numbers. She would have to put off planning the big Thanksgiving gathering. Before she could stop herself, she wondered if she might wind up having to put it off until a different year altogether.

Chapter 3

The spectators made their way from the narrow bleachers through the exit doors. It was quiet in the gym, the grim silence that typically followed a loss for one of Meadow Middle School's sports teams. The basketball team had a long-standing rivalry with Xavier Middle, but in the last several years, Xavier had won every game. That losing streak made Meadow's 49–27 loss today particularly humiliating.

Meg and Sam said nothing as they walked toward the car. They both knew what kind of mood Will would be in when he finished changing out of his uniform and came through the gym's side exit. Neither one of them was looking forward to it. Will wasn't a great basketball player by any measure, but his height and speed helped make him one of the best on the team. He treasured that position. It made up for the fact that he wasn't a good enough athlete to play football, which Meg knew was the sport that mattered most to the kids as they approached high school. It was the only sport that mattered to Will.

It had always been all about football for him. He and his father were rabid Carolina Panthers fans and owned a huge assortment of Panther paraphernalia. The football teams from Duke, UNC, or NC State provided additional hours of tension and jubilation. But Will had to make do with basketball, and he was determined to win at it. A victory made him happy for a week. A loss sent him spiraling into gloom. In most areas of his life, Will was a fairly easygoing child. When it came to this, he was irrational.

Sam got into the backseat and buckled the seat belt. Meg heard him sigh, no doubt anticipating the inevitable unpleasantness of the drive home. Will's innate competitiveness was completely alien to Sam, though he did his best to support his older brother by attending the games and cheering as if he cared. Victories brought rewards for such loyalty—Will might invite Sam into his bedroom to talk or to play video games. Losses brought his older brother's sulking.

Will was the first player to emerge from the locker room, throwing wide the heavy door. He yanked open the car door, slumped into the passenger seat, then reached out and slammed the door as hard as he could.

"Hi, honey," Meg tried.

"Don't even talk to me." He folded his arms across his chest and glared out the window. "Just don't."

Meg turned the car around and drove toward the exit. Most of the crowd had already left, a fair number of them before the game was even over.

"UNBELIEVABLE!" The word exploded from Will "THOSE JERKS CAN SAY THEY'VE BEATEN US FIVE YEARS IN A ROW! DO YOU KNOW HOW BAD THAT IS? DO YOU?"

What Meg and Sam did know was that it was smarter not to answer. They remained quiet as Will continued his tirade. Meg could see Sam in the rearview mirror, fidgeting in his seat. Abruptly, he interrupted. "It's a *bunch of guys with a ball.* Not exactly worth dying over."

Uh-oh, Meg thought, even as she admired her younger son's willingness to put his head in the lion's mouth. Will whipped around in his seat to face Sam, only too glad to be able to target his wrath.

"What would you know about it, you little pus bag? You don't play anything. You're too scared—"

"STOP RIGHT THERE!"

Meg's voice was so loud, it startled even her. Will was about to escalate the personal insults to a point she wasn't going to allow.

"Oh yeah, of course, defend him, like you always do," Will spat out as he turned to face forward again.

No one said another word. Meg was glad when their house finally came into view. As soon as she had parked in the garage, both boys disappeared, headed to their rooms. Meg entered the kitchen to find Lizzie standing at the counter, her eyes red and puffy, sniffling as she spread peanut butter on a banana.

"Sweetheart, have you been crying?" Alarmed, Meg went over to her, putting a hand on Lizzie's arm.

"No!" Lizzie snatched her arm away.

"You want to tell me what's wrong?"

"Nothing. Nothing's wrong." Lizzie looked up at her mother's face, and her resolve crumbled. "It's Emily and Maya. I could just kill them!"

"What happened?"

"It's Facebook stuff. They're on some kind of campaign to get everyone to hate me."

Meg bristled. "Are you serious?"

Lizzie paused, jabbing the knife into the nearly full peanut butter jar so that it stood straight up. "Okay, not *hate* me, maybe, but they're saying a bunch of stuff that makes me look bad. I thought we were good friends, and now it seems like they never considered me a friend. It was all in my mind. I'm nothing to them."

Meg put her arms around Lizzie, and the girl rested her head against her mother's shoulder. She began to cry in earnest. "Why is everybody so mean?" she got out between sobs. "I used to have so many friends, but now it's like every-one's changed."

Meg rubbed Lizzie's back. "Oh, honey, the kids are going through their own stuff. It's not about you, it's about them."

Her daughter pulled away. "You always say stuff like that, Mom. It doesn't mean anything."

"It's really true, if you could just—"

Lizzie grabbed the peanut butter–covered banana and turned to go. "Never mind. I'm sorry I said anything."

"Sweetie—"

"Forget it."

She was gone.

Meg pulled the knife out of the peanut butter, shaking her head. The backbiting among Lizzie's friends had started around seventh grade and now seemed to be constant. Sometimes Lizzie was the target of the gossip, but by the time she got into high school, Meg suspected, her daughter sometimes did a bit of the gossiping herself. It drove Meg crazy, especially since computers and cell phones seemed to have brought the speed of gossip up to the speed of light. Like the news cycle on television, Meg reflected, the popularity cycle seemed to turn over every twenty-four hours.

Upstairs, Will must have emerged from his room as Lizzie was going down the hall, because Meg heard the two of them shouting, something about hogging a DVD. LizzieandWillfighting, just one word, was how Meg thought of these frequent confrontations. She glanced at the clock on the microwave. Two-twelve. There was a lot more of this day to get through.

I will be cool and calm, she resolved, turning to look at the magnet on the refrigerator. It was a small one she had picked up years ago at a local fair, featuring North Carolina's state motto in Latin and English: *Esse quam videri.* To be, rather than to seem. Meg found it comforting, inspiring her not only to try and *appear* calm or wise or whatever she wished she could be at any given moment but actually to *feel* that way. She'd been looking at that magnet a lot lately.

She hurried upstairs to change into her workout clothes, then spent forty minutes on the treadmill in their basement gym. The room had been James's idea, a small area outfitted with the treadmill, a stationary bike, and some free weights, plus a large-screen television. He wound up using it only infrequently, on a Saturday or Sunday morning. Meg tried to put in four days a week, although she hated every minute of it. When she was finished with her workout, luxuriating under the cool stream of the shower, she was surprised to see James enter the bathroom. He didn't say anything but went directly to the sink to wash his hands.

"Hi," she said loudly over the noise of the

44

water. "I thought you were playing golf all afternoon."

"We quit after nine holes."

"Oh, that's a shame—"

He left the room before she could complete her sentence. Meg dragged the washcloth up and down one arm. When it came to whatever it was that was troubling her husband, she was at a total loss. James was clearly going through some problem, but he refused to answer any of her questions. Initially, he had tried distracting her or jollying her along with humor, but he had given that up entirely; he had simply withdrawn. He came home early from the office, or ridiculously late, with no explanations. In the past few weeks, even the children commented on his irritability. She tried to gloss over it with meaningless phrases about how hard he was working.

Meg had repeatedly asked, cajoled, and demanded an explanation. Was he in love with someone else? Having problems at work? Was he sick or addicted to drugs or alcohol? She reminded him that he could tell her anything and she would do anything to help him. She got no response to her entreaties. In fact, he no longer turned to her in bed or showed her any affection at all. It was as if he wanted to be totally alone with his misery. At a loss by this point, Meg decided she would wait it out. Either he would manage whatever was bothering him, or, eventually, she would force him to confide in someone—if not her, then a professional of some kind. She was giving it until New Year's.

When Thanksgiving Day arrived, James's mood hadn't improved, but Meg had pushed ahead with her annual dinner for the neighbors. Eighteen people would be coming over at four o'clock to share in the feast. She had started cooking the previous Sunday, and today she was right on schedule. At noon she began setting the table, which consisted of their dining room table with all four leaves in it, plus two rented tables extending out from either side. Under duress, Lizzie and Will helped spread out the white tablecloths and napkins and carried in chairs from other parts of the house. Sam retrieved all the sterling silver flatware and ornate serving pieces from the basement closet.

Meg liked to do the final setting of the places herself. She enjoyed arranging the silver, china, and crystal, everything sparkling and gleaming. Next she had huge bouquets of flowers in water-filled buckets to arrange and two dozen candles to set out.

"Mom, no one does this anymore, you know." Lizzie paused on her way past the dining room, observing her mother adjusting the positions of multiple sets of salt and pepper shakers. "You don't have to make such a fuss."

Meg laughed. "C'mon, Lizzie, you know I do."

Her daughter smiled. "Yeah, I guess you do. Some people never learn."

Meg hastened back to the kitchen to baste the turkey, which had been roasting in the oven for hours. The juggling act would come later, when she was trying to heat up the enormous quantities of sweet potato pie, plus the peas and mushrooms, and extra stuffing beyond what the bird held. At the same time she needed to mash the cooked potatoes. She consulted her list for the meal. Hors d'oeuvres, spiked punch for adults, soda for children, cranberry sauce, whipped cream for the pies—all ready.

She decided she had earned a break. Pouring a glass of water, she moved to look out the window. The backyard always provided her with a feeling of serenity, its flat expanse of greenery surrounded by tall, shade-providing trees. The family had spent countless evenings grilling and eating dinner on the patio, and those times were among her favorites. She had also put many contented hours into nurturing the flower beds behind the house and along the lawn's perimeter. It gave her tremendous satisfaction to do something with her hands that created so much beauty virtually out of thin air. Try as she might, she couldn't interest any of her children in gardening, and James never had the time or inclination. It didn't bother her, though; she liked having something that was exclusively hers.

She took a long drink of water. Peering out more intently, she saw that the four Adirondack chairs on the far end of the lawn needed a fresh coat of white paint. She made a mental note to add that to the general to-do list.

Unbidden, the thought came to her that she was sick and tired of that list. Of all her lists. Truth be told, she never wanted to lay eyes on her stupid pink leather book with all those idiotic color-coded errands again.

Startled, she turned away from the window. Where had *that* come from? she asked herself. Was she tired of doing what was required to keep the family running smoothly? No, that wasn't it. She had no intention of abandoning any of her family commitments. But she needed to do something different, something more. Her life might be busy, but it wasn't *full*. Maybe it was because the kids were getting older. They still required her time and attention, but it was a different kind of need than when they were little. Something was missing, though. Meg closed her eyes momentarily, willing her thoughts to take a different turn. She sensed that, just by having this conversation with herself, she was letting some kind of genie out of its bottle.

She brought her musings to an abrupt end by reminding herself that, given James's problems, this was hardly the time to be shaking things up.

Anything having to do with her was going to have to wait. The color-coded calendar would remain.

At three o'clock, Meg went upstairs to change, trading the yoga stretch clothes she wore to clean and cook for black pants, black ballet flats, and a cream silk blouse. Quickly, she pinned up her hair and applied makeup.

It was already three-thirty when she came downstairs. It occurred to her that she hadn't seen James since she asked him to take care of the wine selection for dinner. That had to be nearly two hours ago, she thought, frowning. She hadn't expected any help from him on this dinner—although he hadn't insisted, his attitude had made it clear that he didn't want her to do it this year—but she figured he would handle this one small piece. By now he should have brought into the kitchen whatever wine he wanted her to serve.

No doubt he was in his study. She paused outside the door, listening. "James?"

There was no answer. She opened the door. "Are you in here?"

Her husband was seated at his desk with his arms and head down, like a child taking a nap in school. Papers surrounded him. He made no movement at the sound of her entrance.

"James, are you okay?"

Still nothing. Fear rose in Meg.

"*James!* Talk to me!" She started toward him, thinking she could grab the phone on the desk to call 911.

He raised his head.

"Oh, you nearly gave me—" Meg stopped short.

His face was red and wet with tears, and his expression was wild-eyed. Meg noticed a glass and a nearly empty bottle of Scotch on the desk beside him.

"It's all over." His voice was low but harsh.

"What's all over? Why are you getting drunk in here? You're not even dressed yet. We're having people—"

His voice rose. "Forget that. It's all gone, Meg. Our money. Everything."

Meg stared at him, uncomprehending. "What?"

His face crumpled. "I'm so sorry."

The slightest sensation of fear sneaked up Meg's spine. "What on earth are you talking about?"

He reached for the glass and gulped back its contents, then picked up the bottle of Scotch and refilled it. "I broke the cardinal rule. Let my emotions get the better of me. Of all people, I knew better."

Her fear growing stronger, Meg sat down in a chair near his desk. "Please tell me what you're saying."

"I didn't tell you. I *couldn't* tell you." He averted his eyes from hers. "I got fired." He gave a small, bitter laugh. "Well, that's not what they called it, but that's what it was."

"Fired? *You?*" Meg's mind was jumping from one thought to the next. How terrible this was for James. What it meant for the family short term. What he should do to find another job. She caught herself up short; it would do no good to panic. "Okay, let's wait a minute. It's not the end of the world. We'll be okay."

He only looked at hcr.

She frowned. "I can't believe they'd fire someone right before the holidays! When exactly did this happen?"

Another gulp from his glass. "August."

"August?" Meg sat up straighter in the chair. "You've been out of work since August, and you didn't tell me?"

He ran a hand across his forehead tiredly. "I thought I could find another job before I had to tell you. I thought I could fix things."

Questions were piling up in her mind. "But . . . what have you been doing every day when you tell us you're at the office?"

"Nothing. It doesn't matter. Going out, walking, hanging out at Starbucks."

"You've been pretending to go to the office." Meg was stunned, replaying in her mind's eye the months of his dressing for work, taking his briefcase, acting as if everything were the same as always.

"I didn't want the kids to know. Or you. It was humiliating."

Slowly, anger began to crowd Meg's fear. "You didn't tell your wife you were fired because you were *embarrassed?* Are you crazy? I could have helped. I could have done a million things." She was struck by another thought. "And instead of listening to your yelling about the bills, I could have put a halt to all spending. That's what needed to be done." She sank back in her chair. "This is unbelievable, James. In a million years, I never would have expected—"

His expression was pained. "Yeah, well, it was stupid, but you don't know what it feels like to get thrown out of a big job like that, do you?"

She was stunned by the jibe, but she let it pass. Her voice softened. "No, you're right. I don't. I'm just a bit horrified that you would put on such a charade. And that you didn't feel you could trust me enough to tell me." She took a deep breath. "Anyway, we have plenty of savings, and you'll get another job eventually."

He gave her a nasty smile, one she had never seen on him before. "But that wasn't the bad news."

She wasn't at all sure she wanted to hear what else he might say.

"In September I had a great opportunity to invest in a real estate deal. I jumped at it. It was a beautiful deal."

He stopped. Meg swallowed, waiting.

"A few weeks into it, one of the other big investors dropped out. The deal couldn't go forward, and I saw an opportunity to double my returns. I'd make enough so that I could retire, never even have to get another job. I took it. All in."

Meg's stomach clenched. "And . . . ?"

"The guy who put together the deal turned out to be a crook. He stole everything and disappeared."

There was a long silence in the room.

"How much did we lose?" Meg whispered.

"Everything."

Meg barely got the words out. "What's 'everything'?"

Anger at her slowness flashed in his eyes. "Everything means *everything!* All the money we had in the world. Whatever we had as collateral."

"You don't mean the house?" She silently begged him to answer no.

"Of course! The house, the savings, our investments."

"No, you didn't," Meg breathed. "You couldn't have."

Rage and pain flashed across his face as he smacked his hand on the desk. "I could, and I did. I was desperate, and that affected my judgment. That's what did it. McDowall knew I'd been let go, and he played on that, too."

"Is that who took our money? Are they going to find him?"

"They did, but it's not going to help us any. About an hour ago, I talked to another guy who was also an investor. They found McDowall last night in a hotel in Los Angeles. He shot himself. No money anywhere. Nobody knows what happened."

Meg's hand rose to her throat. "Maybe . . ."

He grimaced. "We're never going to see that money again. Like I said, it's over."

Meg sat paralyzed, trying to force her mind to make sense of what she had just heard. No, it wasn't possible. Things like this didn't happen to people like them.

The ongoing flood of emotions seemed to have exhausted James. He spoke quietly. "We have to leave the house. Our cars go back because they're leased. I own the Mustang, so that stays with us. The kids can finish out the semester, since the school bill was paid long ago, but they're done there next month. The big things are obvious." He paused. "You need to understand that all we have is what's left in our checking account, which is about nineteen hundred dollars. And whatever you have in your wallet. I have a hundred and fifty bucks in mine."

He closed his eyes and slowly swung his desk chair around so that his back was to her.

Meg struggled to understand. They had

nowhere to go and money that would last only a few weeks. They were homeless. Destitute. All because James had decided he could cover up getting fired. He had chosen to take every cent they had without even discussing it with her, then handed it over to a crook. No, she corrected herself, he had gone out of his way to *double* his investment.

She thought about the children. If they had no place to live, how would they go to school, private or otherwise? Forget about their having to say goodbye to everything they had ever known in life—their friends, the community in which they lived, their everyday activities. They would lose the very foundation of their lives, which was that they were safe and secure in the world, protected by their parents.

Meg stood, speaking through clenched teeth. "I could kill you right now, James. You've destroyed us. All by yourself. You were too smart, too important, to talk to me about anything you did. You never considered what that could do to your family. If you wanted to play roulette with your own life, that's one thing. But what about the children and me? You thought so little of us, you sacrificed us without a second thought."

James turned his chair to face her. Tears spilled from his eyes as she spoke. "I know," he whispered. "You're right. I don't know what to do to make it up to you."

"I can't imagine that you'll *ever* make this up to us!" She began to tremble, rage and terror threatening to overtake her. "We have *nothing!* James, *how could you?*"

They stared at each other, fury and confusion on her face, misery on his.

The doorbell rang.

"It's the Dobsons." They heard Sam's shout as he raced down the stairs. "I'll get it."

It was four o'clock. Their guests were starting to arrive.

Chapter 4

Bleary-eyed from exhaustion, Meg clasped a mug of steaming coffee with both hands as she made her way around the backyard. It was barely seven o'clock. Now, before the children got up and she had to face whatever this day might bring, she had some time to be alone in the garden. She reached out to touch the cyclamen's heart-shaped leaves, satisfied to see signs of its emerging white flowers. Looking over the remnants of her hydrangea and foxglove blooms, she recalled her small triumphs and disappointments with them over the seasons. Her crocuses would be in full bloom by Christmas, but she wouldn't be there to see them. Maybe it's silly, she thought, but I'll miss this more than the house itself.

She sat down on one of the Adirondack chairs. No need to worry about painting them now.

Yesterday's Thanksgiving meal was probably the hardest thing she ever had to endure. She could barely believe she had gotten through it. Smiling, making small talk, cooking, serving. All the while seeing her husband seated at the head of the table, downing Scotch after Scotch. His exaggerated cheerfulness, obviously fueled by the alcohol, made her wince. Worst of all was watching the children, all three in notably good moods at the same time, a remarkable occurrence. The things she was going to have to tell them— actually uttering the words "We've lost everything, and we have no idea what's to come"— were unimaginable. Meg set her coffee cup on the ground and tightened her robe against the chilly morning air.

After the meal, when everyone had finally left, Meg had the children help clear the table, then, to their apparent shock, dismissed them from further kitchen duty. She needed to be by herself, to let the corners of her mouth release her frozen smile, to fall silent. For the next two hours, she cleaned furiously, her mind blank as she gave herself over to the physical task. She loaded the dishwasher carelessly, dishes banging as she dropped them haphazardly into the slots. Hand-washing the crystal glasses, she squeezed a wineglass so hard the stem snapped, but she ignored the bleeding from her thumb, and after a while it stopped.

Later, when she could find nothing else to clean, she dragged herself upstairs, emotionally and physically drained. James was nowhere to be seen, which was fine with her.

"I'm going to sleep. G'night, kids," she called out from her bedroom doorway.

"Mom?" Sam's voice floated down the hall. It was unusual for her to go to bed without coming into their rooms to say good night.

"Go to bed, Sam," she replied, firmly shutting the door. She hated ignoring her son, but she couldn't face the children. Not tonight.

She peeled off her clothes, dropping them on the bathroom floor before grabbing a nightgown from the hook on the back of the door. What difference did it make what she did with the clothes now? she thought. All her compulsive housekeeping and keeping on top of things had only brought her to this point. Nowhere.

Sliding under the comforter, Meg was so exhausted that she knew, thankfully, she would find the oblivion of sleep quickly. She was wrong. Over and over, she replayed the conversation with James and his actions over the past months. Everything about their life since August was now recast in a completely new light.

It was not a light that reflected flatteringly on her husband. Despite her offering him a hundred openings, he had chosen to keep what was, in terms of a marriage, a monstrous secret. He had lied to her again and again through his silences, his pretense of going to work, his clandestine gambling of all they had.

This couldn't be her husband, her James, the

man who had brought her a cup of coffee every morning since the day they married. Who always filled the house with peonies, her favorite flower, on her birthdays. Who, for years, had designated alone time with each child one Sunday a month to go to a museum or a ball game or wherever his son or daughter might want. He was a straight arrow and honest to a fault. Meg would have bet her life—the lives of her children—that he couldn't have done such a thing. Knowing she would have lost such a bet made her blood run cold.

The sound of the screen door opening brought her back to the moment. She watched James emerge into the morning air, holding his own mug of coffee. He wore the same clothes from the day before and was unshaved, his hair uncombed. It was obvious that he, too, had passed a sleepless night. She wondered if he was feeling hungover from all that Scotch. She hoped so. The sight of her handsome husband usually had a warming effect on her, a combination of love, attraction, and comfort. All that was over. Today she felt only anger and the stabbing pain of betrayal.

"I saw you through the window," he said as he drew closer. "What are you doing out here so early?"

She didn't reply. He sat down on the chair next to her. "Good coffee. Thanks for making it." He glanced down at her feet. "Aren't your slippers getting wet out here?"

She looked over at him in disbelief. "Are we *chatting?*"

His voice suddenly reflected his fatigue. "Look, it won't do us any good to go at each other. We'll have to work this all out, and we might as well do it as a team."

"James, we're not discussing where to go on vacation or whether the kids should take Spanish or French. We're discussing how you deceived me and what you've done to the whole family. We're talking about whether I'm leaving you."

He held up a hand and spoke soothingly. "I know you're angry now, Meg—"

"Don't patronize me." Her tone was icy. "I feel like such a fool, being all chipper to try and cheer you up, feeling sorry for you while you were busy nursing your wounded pride in coffee shops. You know, if we had worked as a 'team,' as you put it, when you lost your job, *that* might have been helpful. I never would have let you risk everything we had, no matter how fantastic the deal was." She stood. "True, you were the one with the high-powered job, the one who made all the money. You were the important one. Nothing I did mattered much. Raising the kids, running our lives—stupid stuff, I guess. Even so, couldn't you have thrown me a bone? Given me a hint what you were going to do?"

She stooped to retrieve her coffee cup. "I'm sorry, but I really can't bear to look at you another minute. We'll have to sit down and go over some things later. Like when we have to get out of the house. And where on earth we're going to go."

James's tone was angry. "Don't twist everything around. I was only trying to spare you and the kids."

"If things had gone your way, that would have been fine. I'd never have been the wiser. It simply didn't occur to you that something might go wrong, did it?" She paused. "Maybe having such a high-powered job isn't always a good thing. The adrenaline of all that risk-taking, the thrill of so much money. It can lead to some pretty terrible consequences."

"You were perfectly happy to spend all that money, as I recall," he said.

She waited a moment to be sure she could sound calm. "Your nastiness aside, none of this is about money, don't you see that? It's about my never being able to trust you again. It's about the fact that our marriage is a big fraud because you're in one marriage, and I'm apparently in another. The person I thought you were would never put his family at risk."

Looking exhausted, he closed his eyes. "I'm the same person I always was."

"Well, James, that kind of makes it worse, you

know? That means I never really understood what kind of person you were."

He looked at her, his gaze hard. "Could we stop all this, please? We have to make some decisions, and we don't have time for you to berate me for hours. What's done is done. We need to move forward."

Her eyes widened. "Wait—you get to do something this terrible, and then you get to dictate how much I can say about it? I'm *annoying* you?" Before he could reply, she turned and walked back to the house, trying to stifle her rage. She refilled her cup in the kitchen and sat down at her desk, her mind racing. There were phone calls to make and lists to compile, lists of awful and humiliating things to do. If only I could go back to my silly to-do lists in my pink leather book, she thought. I'd never complain about it again.

She rummaged through the filing cabinet beneath the desk to assemble an armload of files containing unpaid bills and legal documents. Setting them down, she grabbed a legal pad and a pen. She wrote "cancel" on the top left of the page and started adding whatever came to mind. Cable, newspapers, magazines, cleaning service. Credit cards. She had to find some way to pay off the balances, which were high, but to keep the cards in case they got desperate.

They also owed money at several local shops, many where they knew the owners personally. It wasn't that they were in any great debt to these shops, but Meg typically waited to pay the bills until she had accumulated two or three months' worth. She recalled all the times Mr. Collins at the pharmacy had advised her when the children got sick. His many kindnesses were the reason she did her drugstore shopping at his tiny store instead of the less expensive chain. She must owe him a fair amount on the house account. He would never collect it. Alice, the lovely woman at the dry cleaner, would also go without getting paid on their open account. Glen Richards, their wonderful gardener with whom she had spent so much time discussing what plants worked best where. All these people would be cheated. The mental images made her cringe. She made a note to check on the balances and write IOUs. One day, somehow, she would make good on them.

So many ugly tasks. She jotted down their various insurance policies—medical, life, car. All paid for now, but when the next premiums came due, the policies would lapse, and if one of them got seriously ill or worse, the family would be completely unprotected.

She could see something of the lengths to which James had gone to hide his situation. For the past three months, he had been careful to maintain his usual system of transferring enough money into their checking account so she could pay the bills. What upset her even more was that if she had known the truth, she could have chosen which bills to pay. He had let her go on paying for cable television instead of putting aside funds for more important things.

Her mind drifted to the people they knew around town. She wished with all her heart that she could disappear from Charlotte today, this very minute. She grimaced. To go where? She had several good friends here but no one she would ask to put up a family of five indefinitely. Besides, she could see herself telling her friends that James had lost his job, but sharing that he had lied to her and lost everything in a swindle was a different matter. She knew she could never bring herself to confide that to anyone. Realizing she had to live with this enormous secret made her feel completely alone in the world.

They could go to a motel until their remaining money ran out, but that wouldn't take long. And then what? To make matters worse, she didn't know if she could bear to go anywhere with James ever again. When had he become so obsessed with money and success that he'd given up all perspective? Losing everything, every last penny—it made no sense to Meg. He had no internal brakes, nothing to tell him that things should go so far and no farther. He had lost himself completely.

"Mommy, can you make me pancakes?" Sam

stood in the kitchen doorway in his pajamas, his eyes puffy from sleep.

Meg put the pad facedown on the desk. She would give the children as long as possible to enjoy the life they knew before she yanked it out from under them. "Plain or blueberry, sweetie?"

As the day passed, Meg realized that James was avoiding her. Annoyed, she finally went to seek him out. She found him stretched out in the club chair in his office. He sat immobile, his head resting on the back of the chair, his eyes closed. "I'm awake," he said without moving.

The sight only irritated her more. "What are you doing, holed up in here?" She stood in front of him. "We have about a thousand things that need to be dealt with, and I can't do it all by myself."

He opened his eyes. "What needs to be done?" he asked in a listless tone.

"Well, I made some notes and went over . . ." Meg trailed off as she saw that James was gazing somewhere over her shoulder, clearly not listening. "Is this how it's going to be? I do absolutely everything to clean up this mess? No, James. *No.*" She crossed her arms. "Yes, I see you're sad, you're depressed, your heart is broken. But you and I don't have the luxury of those feelings. We have three children to take care of."

"Kids are resilient. They'll be okay."

Her voice rose. "Whether they'll be okay is another matter, but before that, they have to be *told.* Have you considered how to break this news to them?"

"I don't know." He rubbed his eyes tiredly. "What do you think?"

When had her husband become like this? Meg wondered. He had always been so strong emotionally. Now he seemed incapable of handling any part of the crisis he himself had brought upon them.

She took a breath. "I think we have to tell them the truth. Unfortunately, today. They need to know they can't spend any more money on anything. More important, they need to be told what's coming down the road. What happens to their everyday lives? To their activities, to their friends?"

"Simple enough," James replied. He snapped his fingers. "Poof. All gone." He abruptly leaned forward, grabbing the chair arms angrily. "You want me to be helpful, Meg? Fine! I will take the blame and tell them Daddy wrecked their lives. Will that be sufficient?"

Meg was unmoved by his words. "You *have* wrecked their lives. And yes, that will be sufficient for now. You do all the talking, and I'll be beside you like some philandering politician's wife. We'll present a united front. I'll keep up my end. Just be sure you keep up yours and tell them the truth."

It was nearly five in the afternoon when, seated side by side on the sofa, they called the children to the family room. Sam responded first, plopping down cross-legged on the floor. Lizzie and Will required another few shouts to get them to appear, then they slouched in armchairs, both looking somewhat put upon.

"Why the summit meeting?" Lizzie asked.

"We have some important things to tell you," Meg said. "So please, just listen to Dad until he's done."

She struggled to keep her face neutral as she listened to James lay out the situation. He omitted altogether the part about pretending to go to work for the past four months. His explanation relied on a bad economy and unlucky investments in a way that absolved him from any real responsibility. The children clearly didn't grasp the significance of what he was saying until he started explaining the immediate and painful consequences of not having any money at all. Tense, she watched her two older children's expressions shift from barely attentive to stunned to horrified. Sam's face remained impassive, but the growing intensity of his nail-biting said more than enough.

"*Please* tell me you're kidding, please, please, please!" Lizzie was perched on the edge of her chair, leaning forward, her hands gripping the chair arms. "You *have* to be!"

"Yeah, this is a joke, right?" Will's voice held anger and fear in equal measure.

By this point, Meg's stomach was clenched so tight, she was almost bent in half, her arms crossed over her abdomen. "No," she practically whispered. "No, it's not a joke."

Lizzie sounded frantic. "I don't understand. We don't have any money? *None?*"

James spoke firmly. "That's right. So there will not be one dime going out of this house from now on."

"But I need to pay Megan back for Ali's birthday present, and—"

"Lizzie, listen to me!" James said. "Not one dime. No paying back. No movies, no shopping, no nothing."

"We'll still have our cell phones and laptops, right?"

James shook his head. "Not after tomorrow."

Lizzie was wild-eyed. "You can't do this to us!"

"It'll be all right, honey," Meg soothed.

Her daughter turned to her in fury. "It will not! This is the worst thing that ever happened!"

"How are we going to live?" Will asked. "Will we be able to eat?"

"Your mother and I are taking care of all the details. Don't worry, you won't starve. But we'll be leaving the house in about two weeks, so you'll need to start getting ready. We'll only have my car, the Mustang. We can take just what we can fit into it and not one thing more."

"Are you crazy?" Lizzie shrieked. "That's impossible! We can't live like that!"

"Leaving the house for how long?" Will's face was white.

James paused. "For good. We're not coming back."

Meg tried to soften the blow of his reply. "We're not sure where we're going yet, but it'll be okay. It just won't be in Charlotte. But you have another couple of weeks in school here, which means you'll make it almost to the end of the term. I'm sure we can make arrangements with the school so you can finish your work and get final grades for the semester."

The children sat stock-still, trying to absorb what they were hearing.

"We're leaving school. We're not even staying in Charlotte." Will reviewed what he had just learned in wonderment. "We're poor, and we're literally homeless."

Sam finally spoke, his voice tremulous. "Are we going to die?"

Chapter 5

James sat on the edge of their bed, his head down and his hands clasped between his knees. Meg watched him brace himself for what he was about to do. She almost felt sorry for him. Almost.

She was no happier than he about this decision. There was no place on earth she wanted to go less than her parents' house in upstate New York. But it was the only solution to their problems that made any real sense. Their first priority was to find a place to stay. Only Meg's parents had the room to take them all in, and could be prevailed upon to let them stay indefinitely for free.

Of course, "free" was a relative term, Meg reflected. Payment might not be made in the form of money, but it would most definitely be made. And the cost would be extremely high.

She picked up the phone, punching in the numbers to her childhood home before handing it to James.

He took a deep breath, then stood as he brought the phone to his ear and waited for someone to answer. "Hello, Harlan?" James was trying to sound cheerful, Meg knew, but his voice came out sounding more strangled. "It's James . . . Hobart."

Meg turned away, fiddling with something on their dresser so he wouldn't feel her eyes upon him. She could hear him pace as he talked.

"How are you? Frances doing okay? Good, good."

The brief pauses required for her father's replies told Meg that he was being his usual terse self. James made small talk for a little while longer. Meg noted that her father did not inquire about her or the children.

"Harlan, I need to talk to you about something pretty serious." James was getting down to it but kept his tone casual. "We've had some setbacks here, you know, the economy and such. I'm sure you've been reading about all this. Well, we haven't been immune down here in Charlotte.

"So, what with my firm downsizing and such, turns out we're going to have to do some downsizing ourselves. We bit off a little more than we could chew, I guess, with the house. Foolish in retrospect."

With his last comment, James had purposely handed her father the opening to lecture him. The conversation was becoming increasingly painful for her to listen to, and she knew it was about to get worse.

"Yeah, you're right," James said contritely.

Meg could imagine her father making some self-righteous remark about how this was to be expected when people overreached or didn't follow the tried and true.

"So, Meg and I have been talking. We think the best thing would be if we came to you and I started doing what I should have been doing all along: learning the business."

Meg looked up at her husband. Getting that out must have nearly killed him. While she was glad that he was finally dealing with some of the ugliness his mess had created, at the same time, his groveling was making her cringe in sympathy.

"That's right, Harlan, I am dead serious. It's time for us to get settled into a solid business that we can depend on. Those are the ones that last, no matter what. Like you always said. Heck, I'm definitely looking forward to doing some-thing *real* instead of pushing papers all day. But we'd need to lean on your generosity a bit. You know, maybe staying with you until we get our feet on the ground up there."

James listened as his father-in-law responded.

"Unfortunately, in this market, we won't get anything out of the house. We put a lot of money into it, and I'm not hopeful we'll make it back. So, no, we don't have a whole lot of capital, as they say."

Meg wasn't surprised that her husband chose to finesse the issue of their losing the house. She couldn't really imagine him saying that they would be leaving with only the shirts on their backs. The conversation went on for another minute or so before he brought it to a close.

"Yes, you're absolutely right. Yes. Well, okay, then, that sounds fine. What time tonight? Good. Send my best to Frances in the meantime."

James pressed the off button and put down the phone. He turned to Meg. "You have to call back tonight at seven. He said your mother would handle any 'domestic arrangements,' as he so quaintly put it. She's out now."

"Will he give you a job?"

"Yes. He said it was about time I'd come to my senses."

"James, I know how hard that—"

"Oh, cut it out." His face contorted with fury. "You must have really enjoyed that. For the rest of your lives, you and your parents can hold it over my head, how I came crawling to them for help. *Begged* them to take in my family and give me some crummy job. Happy now?"

Meg took a step back in surprise. "You think that makes me happy?"

"I *know* it does." James left the bedroom, slamming the door behind him.

Whatever sympathy Meg had felt for him vanished. He viewed himself as a victim, she realized, and somehow she was going to be the villain. He was writing his own script about what had happened. Unfortunately, she could see that it wasn't going to have much to do with the truth.

Meg left the room only to be met by the sound of Lizzie crying. Ever since yesterday, when they told the children the news, Lizzie had been virtually holed up in her bedroom. She hadn't come down for dinner, and the dirty cereal bowl and spoon in the sink this morning were the only evidence that she had eaten anything between then and now. Periodically, Meg would knock on her daughter's door, but all she got in the way of a response was "Go away!"

She tried again with a gentle knock. "Lizzie? Please let me talk to you."

To Meg's surprise, she received silence in reply. She took that as an invitation and opened the door a few inches. "Can I come in?"

The only answer was Lizzie's sniffling. Meg entered to find her daughter stretched across the bed on her stomach, her face turned toward the wall.

"Oh, honey, I know this is so, so hard," Meg said.

Lizzie kept her face averted, and her voice was muffled by sobs. "No, you don't. You don't know anything. You may have grown up in some stupid little town, but nobody made you leave your house and everything you owned. Nobody destroyed everything you worked so hard to build—friends, your social life—everything." She turned her face toward Meg. It was red and tear-stained. "How could you do this to me?" Her voice grew louder. "Why did you let this happen? You have three children. Didn't you think about us at all?"

"Your father and I—"

"I can't understand how you and Daddy could be so stupid. And selfish. You didn't save anything or have any kind of plan. Boom, just like that, our lives are gone."

"There's a lot you don't understand about all this."

Lizzie regarded her mother dully. "I understand that I hate you. You've ruined my life, like, literally, *ruined* it." She turned her face to the wall again. "I wish I were dead. Leave me alone. I never want to see you again."

Meg stood there for a moment, trying to imagine what this all felt like to her daughter. Then she left the room.

As she made her way down the hallway, she saw the door to Sam's room was open. Peering in, she froze. Her nine-year-old sat on the floor in the center of the room, surrounded by a huge array of boxes and bags full of his collections. Meg watched silently as he lovingly examined some tiny rubber action figures.

His stuff. The stuff that made him the quirky, sweet kid he was. She hadn't thought about how he would have to abandon all the things he had collected. All the things that somehow represented to him security and control in a scary world. How could they ask him to do that? The other two children would have to part with clothes and gadgets and a range of things that were bound to be painful to them. But Sam would have to let go of a part of himself that he wasn't ready to give up. He shouldn't have to.

He saw her standing in the doorway and smiled. "Hi, Mom."

Of the three children, Sam was the only one who hadn't displayed anger toward Meg or James. After their gathering in the family room, Will had left the house yelling out angrily that he would be at Leo's as he slammed the door behind him. He wasn't supposed to leave home without a parental okay, but Leo lived within walking distance, and under the circumstances, no one was about to stop him. This morning he had sullenly allowed Meg to cook him scrambled eggs and toast, retreating with the plate to his room so he wouldn't have to sit with her in the kitchen. Apparently, he wasn't speaking to his parents any more than he had to.

Sam had been very quiet, but it was a different kind of quiet. He was clearly afraid, and he seemed to Meg more fragile. He had spent much of the morning in her presence, practically following her from room to room, trying to be helpful in any way he could. It was as if he needed to be with her but was trying not to add to the misery and disruption in the house.

Meg forced a smile to match his. "Hi, pumpkin."

He got up and went over to his desk, retrieving a crumpled pile of dollar bills there. "I saved this from my allowance and stuff. It's eighteen dollars. I thought maybe you and Daddy could use it."

"No, no, Sam." The words caught in her throat. "That's very nice. But you keep it."

She turned away before he could see her face. Hurrying down the stairs, tears burning her eyes, she went out to the backyard and got as far from the house as she could before bursting into long, loud sobs. It was the first time since all this had started, she realized, that she had cried. Now that she had started, she wasn't sure she would be able to stop. She cried for the children and for her marriage. She cried with fear, having no idea what the next months would bring. She cried at the realization that the security of her life had been such a flimsy illusion.

Much later, when she couldn't cry another tear, she stood, exhausted, and made some resolutions. She wouldn't let the children see her get down. No matter how furious she was at James, they would maintain the best possible relations in front of them. Last, she wouldn't rely on her husband to get them out of their financial straits because the likelihood that he could tolerate working for her father was pretty much zero.

At exactly seven o'clock that evening, Meg sat down at the kitchen table to call her mother. If Meg's mother had said to call at seven, she expected to receive the call at seven, not 7:01. Tardiness as a symptom of weak character had been a frequent topic of discussion between her parents during Meg's childhood. Whatever else tonight's conversation might bring, she wanted to eliminate that subject as a possibility.

The phone rang and rang. Meg could picture her mother in the kitchen, washing up after supper, unhurriedly drying her hands on a dish towel before reaching for the wall-mounted telephone.

"Hello." A flat statement without expectation.

That one word was enough to make Meg flinch. "Mother, hi, it's Meg."

"Hello, Margaret. Didn't hear from you yesterday on Thanksgiving, but I understand you've gotten yourself in a lot of trouble down there."

Double points, Meg thought grimly. The reprimand for the missed call and the put-down both in one sentence. The fact that her mother still insisted on calling her by her given—and hated—name of Margaret was just the usual icing on the cake.

"I'm very sorry we have to bother you like this.

I really appreciate you and Dad letting us stay with you for a while."

"I'm hardly surprised it came to this, dear. That big-deal firm James worked for, all those fancy companies, you just knew they were going to come to no good. Dishonest cheats, all of them."

"I guess" was all Meg could get out.

Her mother's pinched tone couldn't disguise her satisfaction. "If you'd listened to your father and me when we told you to come back home after you two married—well, I don't have to tell you that you wouldn't be in this predicament now."

Meg forced a jovial tone. "But look how it's working out—James will be joining the family business after all."

"We'll see," her mother said primly. "Frankly, I wonder if he can handle going from those expensive suits and expense-account lunches to real life."

Meg wanted desperately to move the conversation in another direction. "This will be a chance for the kids to spend time with you. You can all get to know one another a lot better."

Her remark was met with silence.

Meg tried not to feel hurt. "They're nice kids, Mother."

"Just remember, Margaret, I brought up one child, and I'm not bringing up any more," her mother said. "Once was enough."

"Don't worry," Meg said sharply. "No one expects you to do anything at all for them." She caught herself. Getting into an argument wouldn't help matters. "You're doing plenty just letting us come. We really appreciate it, and we'll stay out of your hair."

"Fine. The three of them will sleep in the spare room, and you and James can have your old room."

"Of course. Thank you." Meg knew there wasn't any other choice, but the scenario filled her with dread.

"When are you coming?"

"It'll be a couple of weeks. Can I let you know when we get closer?"

"I can't have you calling me that morning to tell me you'll be showing up for lunch."

"No, no, Mother, I'll give you plenty of notice. How about if I call you next week and give you a firm date?"

"Fine. Call next Friday, at seven, like tonight."

"Yes, I will."

There was a pause. "I hope you two have learned a lesson. You were riding so high. And look at you now. To be your age and have to come home to live with your parents because you have no money . . ."

"Yes, well, these things happen," Meg said through clenched teeth. "So—goodbye. Talk to you next week."

She set down the telephone. Then she folded her arms on the table and buried her head in them. Today she and James had made only the first small installment of the many payments yet to come.

Over the next two weeks, Meg was grateful that the job of closing up the house kept her constantly busy. It made it easier for her to ignore any thoughts about how much she loved the landscape painting hanging in the living room, or the art deco perfume bottle James had given her one year for their anniversary. Early on in her marriage, she had done a lot of baking and, over the years, had amassed a large array of cooking and decorating tools. As she tossed the pans and pastry brushes into shopping bags, she fought to avoid recalling the birthday cakes and holiday pies she had made, the cupcakes for school events.

They weren't in a position to pay for storage, and her parents had little extra space, so she filled every old box and bag in the house with items to toss, attempt to sell, or donate to charity. Faced with the mountains of papers relating to the children's past schoolwork and art, she dedicated one plastic storage box to each of them and steeled herself to pare down the memories to fit. Vans pulled up to the house to haul away sofas, chairs, lamps, tables. Any money they made from whatever might be salable would go directly to the credit card companies—the most immediate problem—and the rest to the small-store owners with whom they had unpaid accounts. Although she and her family desperately needed money, it was critical to Meg to know she would take care of these local people after all. When she informed James of this, he nodded in agreement, a sign to her that at least some remnant of his basic decency had survived.

She boxed and shipped the family photo albums to her parents' house, plus some small items that held sentimental value for her. She told each child to pack two cartons of whatever they deemed important and sent those along as well. Despite the cost, some things were simply beyond her resolve.

They had under a week left until the day they would leave the house for good. Meg kept her eye on the deadline, forcing herself to remain numb to the sight of her life being dismantled. The children, on the other hand, made their feelings abundantly clear. Sam retreated further into himself, while the other two remained angry and sullen. Lizzie continued to do the most crying and yelling at Meg, while Will glowered, watching television alone in the basement playroom or disappearing into his bedroom, refusing to answer any questions. Meg told the children that they were responsible for clearing out their rooms, so they could choose what to keep. As she disposed of the things they'd left behind, she tried not to look at Lizzie's bags of favorite childhood dolls, and sadly emptied the cartons into which Will had carelessly tossed his basketball trophies and football memorabilia. At the last minute, she retrieved his favorite skateboard from a box; somehow they would make space for it in the car.

One of the few times she broke down was the afternoon she spent in the basement, sorting through Christmas ornaments. She had collected a few new ones each year and any time they traveled, ever since James and she had gotten married. Each one held a special memory. The lights, tinsel, angels, and decorations to adorn windows and doors—it was unbearable. Christmas was so soon, it killed her to think they would miss having it one last time in the house. Of all the holidays, it was by far her favorite and the one she made the biggest fuss over. Everything about it was exciting to her: wrapping presents, baking cookies, filling the house with the sound of carols and silly singing Santas. When she was growing up, her parents had little appreciation for a holiday they believed had degenerated into "nothing but an excuse to get people to spend their money." They would go to church and put up a small tree, the cheapest one they could find, which Meg would decorate with her handmade paper cutouts. On

Christmas morning she would receive something useful, like socks or mittens. It was a joyless event all around. As an adult on her own, Meg did her best to create a virtual festival, with huge, lavish presents and mountains of food.

Now she was facing another holiday season back in her parents' house. They would approve of the fact that the kids would get little or nothing, but only because Meg and James could no longer afford big gifts. Or small ones, for that matter. Meg's tears were a mixture of sorrow and bitterness.

Whether James was thinking about any of this, only he could say. He spent most of the time in his study, even sleeping on the couch there at night. Meg asked him to handle the dismantling of that room and all the bookshelves' contents throughout the house, which he did without comment. Often he went out around dinnertime. It was obvious he wanted to avoid eating with the family. Meg would have liked to avoid those meals herself, with her two older children either sulking or complaining and Sam growing progressively more nervous and fearful. But she wasn't about to run out on them, and her resentment toward James grew deeper each time he failed to appear. She wasn't sure what to make of the hard set of his mouth when he did address her. Clearly, he was angry, but whether it was at her, himself, or the world, she couldn't quite say.

Neither of them made any attempt to discuss it—or anything else beyond what was absolutely necessary.

The tension in the house only increased as all three children realized their ideas of what would fit in one suitcase were far off the mark. There were multiple sessions of Meg sitting on someone's bed as that child wept or raged over parting with ever more precious items. Even Sam yelled through his tears when he had to make the impossible choice between the large bags of tiny stuffed-animal key chains and assorted plastic aliens. "It's too much, Mommy," he cried. "Please don't make me do this."

Her heart ached for all three, and she suggested they each pack a second, smaller bag if they were willing to have it beneath their feet for the entire car trip. She hoped she was doing the right thing: It was roughly seven hundred miles to Homer, New York, with the kids cramped in the backseat. They gladly agreed with her idea to sit with their own pillows and blankets; that would keep them warm and comfortable without taking up trunk space. However, their pleasure dissipated when she pointed out that they also needed to wear their heaviest jackets and warmest clothes because the weather would be far colder going north. She didn't mention that they would nonetheless still be underdressed, as there had never been a need to outfit them for snow and ice. The blankets were necessities for the drive. When they got upstate, somehow she would have to provide them with warmer gear.

In some ways, it was a relief when the day they were to leave finally arrived. Meg didn't think she could stand much more. They were all exhausted and emotionally drained from disposing of their old lives. The children got out of bed as soon as she woke them, and they moved about quietly, speaking only when necessary. Everyone ate a quick breakfast, and, as planned, they were ready to go by ten o'clock. Meg knew there was no point, but she washed the breakfast dishes and sponged down the counters. She couldn't bring herself to leave the house looking abandoned and uncared for.

As she passed through the kitchen on her way out, she noticed that she had removed everything from the refrigerator door except the magnet with the state motto. Somehow she had overlooked it. *To be, rather than to seem.* She slipped it into her pants pocket.

James's 1969 white Mustang was his pride and joy, what Meg called his favorite toy. He had bought it for himself as a reward when he had been hired for the job in Charlotte at a salary far higher than what he had been receiving at his previous company. Initially, he had driven the car a fair amount, but now he took it out only for an occasional spin, unwilling to forgo the conveniences of his BMW. Although the Mustang had two doors, it was designed to hold four people; the back had a bucket seat design, with a rise in the center of the seat and on the floor. Without a lot of interior room, it was barely comfortable for four, much less five. It had never been James's intention to drive the car anywhere with his entire family at one time, much less on an extended trip. No one was surprised when the backseat proved miserably tight for three people with small suitcases, pillows, and blankets.

It was also predictable that, as the youngest, Sam would be forced by his siblings to sit in the middle. "Why do I have to sit on the hump?" he asked unhappily.

"Because you *do,* that's why," Will said.

"Look, kids, you're packed in there like sardines," James said. "If you want to jettison some stuff, it might be a little better."

Unwilling to relinquish any of the little they had left, they immediately stopped complaining, while Meg and James grimly struggled to get everything in the trunk. Meg was keeping her fingers crossed that the car would be up to making the trip.

It was a sunny day, the blue sky streaked with patches of wispy clouds. There was total silence as they pulled out of the driveway. Meg noticed that neither James nor the children looked back at the house. She guessed that for them, as for her, it would have been too much to stand.

The leased BMWs had built-in navigation systems, but no such thing existed when the Mustang was manufactured. They would be using the driving directions Meg had printed out while they still had their computers, plus some old AAA maps. She removed the Southeastern States map from her handbag and unfolded it.

"Take the next left," she intoned, imitating the voice from her car's navigation system. "Drive twelve million miles. Then, destination is on the right."

No one smiled. All three children got out their iPods—with no monthly charges, they were among the few electronic gadgets they had been able to keep—and retreated into their music. Meg looked out the window at the streets of Charlotte flying by. If they had been leaving under different conditions, she and James would have been sharing memories and making comments on what they were passing. Instead, James stared straight ahead as he drove. No matter how things were resolved, she knew in her heart she wouldn't be coming back here. This life was finished.

Lizzie and Will started fighting before they got to Winston-Salem, and everyone was short-tempered by the time they pulled onto I-81, the highway on which they would be doing most of the driving. The route took them through Virginia.

Thinking it would make for a pleasant interlude, Meg had planned a stop at Luray Caverns. If they had to make this trip, she figured, at least the kids could see a few interesting sights and learn something.

The one-hour tour of the underground caverns didn't go well. The two older children complained continually that they were cold and bored. Sam dragged his feet, saying he had a stomachache. James was either snapping at them to keep quiet while the guide was talking, or fruitlessly trying to interest them in the difference between stalactites and stalagmites. The less they listened to him, the more annoyed he became at their unwillingness to appreciate the beauty surrounding them.

It was a relief for all of them when they eventually checked into a motel for the night, the cheapest one they could find that seemed reasonably clean and safe. The children piled onto one of the beds and turned on the television. Meg took a shower so she could have ten minutes of peaceful solitude, the same reason, she guessed, that James went alone to fill the car with gas. She dried herself as best she could with the small, rough towel provided as she thought about what would be the least expensive dinner options.

The next morning the children were groggy, surprisingly unwilling to relinquish their scratchy blankets and get out of their uncomfortable bed.

Meg and James dressed and split up so that one could get the free coffee and doughnuts from the motel's lobby while the other kept an eye on the children. It was nearly eleven before they checked out, and the amount of complaining and stops demanded from the backseat escalated considerably from the previous day. It was a slow, unpleasant ride under a cold and gray sky all the way to Pennsylvania.

When she had planned this drive back in Charlotte, Meg estimated that they would reach Lancaster County that afternoon. She knew it was an area with a big Amish population. Neither she nor the children knew much about the Amish, and this would be a wonderful chance to learn a little bit. It was Sunday, with few things open, but her research at home had turned up a film about the Amish with regular Sunday screenings. At least they could see that much.

Meg didn't recall what time the day's last showing of the film was, but when she saw it was four o'clock as they pulled off the highway, she knew they were probably too late. This detour had been a bad idea, she thought, but they might as well check on the movie and see whatever sights there were along the way. She directed James to an address in the town of Intercourse, the name of which provided Lizzie and Will with numerous snickers. It had snowed earlier in the week, evident in the graying snow and patches of ice on the sidewalks and roads. On the local Route 340, they passed closed shops that obviously catered to tourists the rest of the week. The town appeared deserted.

When they arrived at the theater, it was closed.

James exhaled in annoyance. "This was a waste of time."

"Turns out that's true," Meg said, maintaining a level tone. "So we'll go back to the highway and move on." She thought about how late it was. "Actually, we should probably find a motel around here for tonight."

James pulled the car back onto the road. It was completely dark now, and the evening brought with it the coldest weather they had encountered on their trip. Meg retrieved a penlight from her bag to consult her AAA guidebook. Busy flipping through the section on lodgings, she didn't notice when James somehow took a wrong turn and left the main road. It took her awhile to notice that they were driving on unlit country roads, probably far from an area where they might find a motel.

"Where are we?" she asked James. "I can't see any street signs."

"How should I know? I'm retracing my steps back to 283."

"No, this isn't the way back. We definitely didn't come this way."

"Mom's right," Will offered. "There were stores."

"Are we lost?" Sam asked.

James's voice rose. "No, we are not lost! Would everybody just relax? Meg, can you see where we are on one of those maps?"

"No, I don't have anything with this much detail."

"If I had my navigation system—"

"Well, you don't," Lizzie interrupted. "Suck it up. *We* don't have anything we want, either."

"Watch it, Lizzie," James warned.

"It's really, really dark here," Sam whispered loudly to Will.

"It's called night, you idiot" was Will's retort.

"All three of you keep quiet!" James ordered. "Not another word." He braked at a stop sign. They could drive straight or take roads veering slightly right or left. There was also a tight hairpin turn to the extreme right, with the road sloping sharply down. He pointed in that direction to Meg. "Maybe that'll take us back."

She nodded. "Might as well try it."

James put his foot down on the gas and turned the wheel hard to the right.

"Ow, get off me!" Will yelled as the car leaned sharply to the side and Sam was pressed up against him.

Lizzie leaned forward to yell back at Will. "It's not his fault, stupid."

"Who asked you?" he snapped.

Between their raised voices and the closed car

windows, none of them heard the horse-drawn buggy coming up the hill. Its flashing red lights were hidden from their view until it came around a curve in the road. In the brief moments it took for the car to make the turn and start downhill, the buggy was almost upon them. James braked hard, but ice on the road caused the car to swerve violently. Realizing that he was within split-seconds of hitting the horse head-on, James jerked the steering wheel to the right as hard as he could.

The Mustang responded, and its headlights illuminated the telephone pole on the side of the road just before they crashed into it.

Chapter 6

Lizzie and Sam both screamed. Will flung up his arms to protect his head. Meg felt the seat belt jerk her body back. The windshield shattered, spraying glass in all directions. The sickening noise of the collision and breaking glass were matched by the violent jolt of the impact, so jarring that it left Meg terrified.

She felt James's shoulder hit her hard as he leaned—or was thrown—toward her.

For a moment everyone was too stunned to speak. Through the open windshield, the cold night air rushed into the car.

"Mommy!" Sam's fearful cry broke the silence. "I got hurt. Will hurt me!"

"Mom, what happened?" Lizzie's tone was frantic.

Meg told herself to get control. She couldn't afford to panic. "What is it, Sam? Will, Lizzie, are you okay?"

"I'm fine," Will said.

"My head hurts," Sam whimpered. "Will hit me with his elbow really hard."

"It was an accident! There's nothing wrong with you!"

"Lizzie?"

Her daughter was beginning to cry. "I want to go home."

Meg turned to look at James. His face was white. Blood trickled down his temple from a cut on his head, and she saw several other slashes on his face and neck from the pieces of glass that seemed to be everywhere. "James?"

"I'm all right." He spoke quietly. "You?"

The door on Meg's side was yanked open from the outside, startling all of them. "You folks okay in there?"

A man in a black coat and black hat with a wide, flat brim peered in, an anxious expression on his face. He had a full brown beard but no mustache, and dark hair with bangs cut straight across his forehead. The man driving the buggy, Meg realized. An Amish man, of course.

"You need to get to a hospital?" He had an accent that Meg interpreted as something between German and Dutch.

James leaned forward to talk to him across Meg. "Just a little banged up. But thanks."

The children were staring at the man with mild fright. He looked them over, noting the heavy quilts surrounding the three. "You were lucky, wrapped up like that. Cushioned the blow, I'd guess."

"My brother hit me in the head," Sam volunteered.

"Shut up," Will shot back.

The man turned his attention back to James. "Do you have people nearby? You live here?"

"No, we're not from here," James said. "We were looking for a motel to spend the night. We got lost."

"Ah, well." The man nodded, thinking. "You best come home with me, then. In the morning you can decide what to do." He straightened up. "I'll bring the horse closer."

As soon as he moved away from the car, Will burst out, his cry urgent. "No way! We're not going to that freak's house!"

"He's totally creepy." Lizzie was just as vehement. "You just know their house is disgusting. You *can't* make us go there."

James closed his eyes and spoke slowly. "Our car is destroyed, and we have no place to sleep. So we're going to accept this very kind stranger's offer, and you are going to be perfect little angels. Do I make myself clear?"

Silence from the back.

"I understand, Daddy," Sam finally offered.

"Be quiet, you little suck-up," Lizzie hissed.

"Now, then, let's see if we can get you out of there." They heard the man's voice before they saw his face at the window again.

Meg shifted her body carefully among the

jagged shards of glass scattered about. She realized that she, too, had a number of stinging cuts, some still bleeding.

But she was weak with relief to see that the children had escaped any real injury. Sam was already developing a lump on his forehead from Will's elbow, and it would doubtless be much bigger by the next day. Lizzie's left foot was bothering her; she must have smacked it on something, but it didn't seem serious. Thank goodness for those quilts and pillows, Meg thought.

Shivering in the icy night, the children clutching their quilts around them, the family surveyed the wreckage of their car. James had nearly managed to avoid the telephone pole, but his side of the car hadn't quite cleared it. The front left had smashed into the pole and was pushed in like an accordion. Thinking of their narrow escape, Meg felt faint.

"Let's get you out of the cold," the man said.

One at a time, he helped them up into the buggy, James and Will in the front seat, the others in back. A thick leather top kept the wind off them, but inside it was far from warm. Meg put an arm around Sam and Lizzie, who slumped miserably against her. James wrapped his arm around Will's shoulders, and, uncharacteristically, his son allowed it.

"My name is David Lutz." He got in next to James and picked up the leather reins. He made a slight clicking sound, and the horse began to trot. "I'll send my sons back for your bags. You need to get the car towed."

"We can't thank you enough, Mr. Lutz," James said loud enough to be heard over the horse's trotting.

"I don't know what we would have done," Meg added.

David Lutz turned his head so his words could be heard more easily. "No. I thank you. You put yourselves in danger so you wouldn't hit me. We just need to see you all get taken care of and get a good rest."

He faced front once again and said nothing else for the rest of the ride.

It was too dark to see much along the narrow roads. The houses and farms were spread far from one another, with few lights on. My poor kids, Meg thought, still comforting Lizzie and Sam. On top of everything else, a car accident. Now this incredibly strange rescue.

Abruptly, the horse turned in to a long dirt road leading to a house, then came to a halt. The shades on the first floor were drawn, but faint light could be seen outlining the edges.

"Wait here," David Lutz said. "I'll be right back with some help."

He disappeared into the house. The children disembarked on their own. As Meg and James began to ease themselves down from the buggy, the front door to the house opened, and David Lutz emerged with two teenage boys, one taller than the other but both dressed identically. Despite the cold, they wore only long-sleeved dark blue shirts and black pants with suspenders. They hastened over to assist Meg and James.

"You are hurt?" The shorter boy, holding his hands out to Meg, had the same lilting accent as his father.

"Just a little shaken up," she said, grateful for his arm as she stepped down onto the icy ground.

"Come inside. My mother is making you something to eat."

All three of their children waited until Meg and James entered the house first, not out of politeness, Meg knew, but so they could hide behind them. They entered a large, dimly lit room that contained a kitchen on the far end and a huge wooden dining table surrounded by what might have been twenty chairs. The furniture was solid but simple. There were no decorations on the walls other than a calendar and a stitched sampler with words that Meg guessed to be German. She realized kerosene lamps were providing what little light there was. On the wall next to her, she saw a long, low bench and, above it, hooks mounted on a narrow piece of wood, each hook occupied by a black coat or cape. Some hooks also held either the same type of hat David was wearing or what appeared to be women's black bonnets. On the opposite side of the room, Meg saw wooden chairs and a sofa with padded blue cushions. Behind them were additional chairs next to several folding tables set up with crayons and paper, half-done puzzles, and a game of Monopoly still in progress. Everything in the room appeared old and worn from use but immaculately clean.

Behind her, Meg heard Will whisper. "Can you believe this place?"

Lizzie whispered back. "Kill me now."

Meg shot them a warning look.

A woman stood by the stove. Short and slender, she was dressed in a mauve-colored dress and a black apron. The dress came down to the middle of her calves, and below that she wore dark black stockings but no shoes. Her hair was all but hidden beneath a white cap whose strings hung down, untied.

At the sound of people entering the house, she turned. Her face was free of makeup, her features plain. It seemed to Meg that she could have been anywhere from thirty to fifty.

"Hello. Welcome to our house." The woman smiled warmly. "I'm Catherine. Would the children like tea or hot chocolate? I'm warming some stew, but that will take a little more time."

There was an enormous covered pot and a teakettle on the stove behind her.

"You're very kind," James said. "Thank you."

"Come." David Lutz ushered them over to the table, waving to the two boys to pull out chairs for their guests. Lizzie, Will, and Sam took seats, all three keeping their gazes down. Meg wondered if she looked as ill at ease as they did. She couldn't believe how nervous she felt, afraid she would say or do something inappropriate or even offensive to these people. She cast about to recall anything at all she might know about the Amish.

"These are two of my sons, Jonathan and Eli," David continued.

Both boys said a bright "hello."

"Oh, I'm so sorry. I feel ridiculous," Meg said. "We haven't even told you our names. I'm Meg Hobart."

"James Hobart." He reached out to shake David Lutz's hand.

They looked expectantly at their children, who mumbled their names, trying to avoid meeting anyone's eyes.

"I'll get some things for you to clean off this blood," Catherine said. She disappeared through a doorway.

Their host turned to James and Meg. "I sent my daughter to bring a doctor we know. He should look at all of you."

"Oh, no, you don't have to—" James protested.

David held up a hand. "While we wait, tell me if I can get you something."

"We have to make some calls about the car," James said. "We don't have cell phones on us, though. Do you have a phone I could use?"

"There is a telephone outside in the shed," David told him. "We don't keep one in the house."

The three Hobart children looked astonished.

James nodded. "Thank you. I appreciate it."

"Jonathan." David addressed his son. "You and Eli see what you can get out of their car. Their suitcases and such. Come. I'll tell you where."

He quickly strode out the front door as the boys grabbed black jackets from the hooks and followed. Able to see them a little better now, Meg judged Jonathan to be around eighteen, while Eli looked closer to fourteen. They both had blond hair in the same bowl-shaped haircut as their father.

It struck her that Eli was probably between Lizzie and Will in age. Somehow that didn't seem possible. It wasn't just the clothes and haircut. Maybe it was his demeanor or the open and direct way he spoke to them. She wasn't quite sure what the quality was that made him so different, but there was definitely something. She tried to imagine her children responding so quickly and respectfully to her. The mental image almost made her laugh aloud. Suddenly, she realized that the incongruity of her children and respectful behavior wasn't funny at all. Not even a little.

Meg rubbed her eyes, exhausted. When Lizzie was little, Meg would tuck her into bed at night and, trying to get her resistant child to go to sleep, say that it had been a big day and now it was time to rest. Lizzie would always shake her head and demand, "*More* big day!" The phrase had become something of a family joke.

"Too much big day," Meg said softly.

Lizzie overheard her mother's comment. "Darn right, too much big day," she muttered. "*Way* too much."

Meg looked over to see Catherine Lutz enter the room with several small towels and washcloths. She put them down on the table, then went back to the stove, pausing to stir the contents of the pot. "Almost ready," she said, peering in at what was no doubt the stew she had mentioned.

Meg had no desire to eat. All she wanted to do was crawl into a bed somewhere and sleep. She glanced at James. He looked as if he was struggling to keep his eyes open. Everything that had led up to this minute seemed to be catching up with them. Leaving the house, making this trip and dreading the day they reached their destination, everyone's bickering, and then this crash. Meg wanted to sleep for a hundred years so she didn't have to think about any of it. She would bet James felt the same way.

The children, on the other hand, were seated at the table looking bored but fully awake. Will was rhythmically kicking the rungs of his chair. Sam had folded his hands on the table in front of him and was turning them this way and that, intently examining them. Lizzie sat slouched over, an elbow on the table, her head resting on her hand. All this might catch up with them later, but for now Meg felt certain they would be fine sitting here, eating—or rudely turning up their noses at —whatever this lovely woman was nice enough to serve them.

Catherine came to the table with a large bowl of warm water. She dipped two worn but clean washcloths into the water, wrung them out, and handed them to Meg and James. For the first time, Meg looked closely at her own arms and saw the thin streaks of blood.

These are truly kind people, Meg thought as she dabbed at her cuts with the warm cloth. Imagine opening your house to help a bunch of strangers who had almost run you over. Taking a quick look at her sullen children, she hoped the Lutzes wouldn't come to regret it.

Chapter 7

Meg opened her eyes to see an overcast day through the panes of an unfamiliar window. The gray sky gave no clue whether it was morning or afternoon. Trying to clear her head, she stared at the short beige curtains framing the window. As she shifted position on the bed, she let out an involuntary groan. Every inch of her body hurt.

It all came back to her at once. The accident, the buggy ride to the Lutz household, James going outside to the shed where the Lutzes kept a telephone so he could call a tow truck. His second call had been to the insurance company, and Meg had breathed a sigh of relief knowing that their policy was paid up until the first of the year.

When the doctor arrived, Meg had been surprised to see that he wasn't Amish, but he was a friend of the Lutz family. He examined them all to check for broken bones or signs of trauma and prescribed ice for the bump on Sam's head and the bruise on Lizzie's foot. As the doctor removed slivers of glass from the cuts on James and Meg, he warned them that they might feel a bit battered in the morning. Reassured that they had ibuprofen in their possession, he left, refusing James's offer of payment.

After that, Catherine Lutz had served bowls of steaming beef stew with warm home-baked bread and butter, tall glasses of water, and hot tea. Meg hadn't realized she was hungry until she caught the aroma of the food put in front of her. Although she and James quickly finished their portions, she saw that her children ate only the bread, making disgusted faces at one another behind Catherine's back as soon as they tasted the thick stew.

After she finished eating, Meg picked up her bowl and glass and came around to Will, who was about to step away from the table. "Clear your dishes and push in your chair," she whispered.

His startled expression confirmed that he hadn't thought of doing either, but he carried his plates to the kitchen counter. Lizzie and Sam followed suit.

Catherine told Lizzie she could share a room with her daughter, Amanda, who was sixteen. She had gone to a friend's house nearby, but she would be back later. Will and Sam would be given the bedroom of the Lutzes' seventeen-year-old son, who was away. They all grabbed their bags, which had been retrieved and neatly lined up near the door, and trooped upstairs, Lizzie limping and complaining about the pain in her foot. Only a few kerosene lamps lit the steps and hallways. It was a large upstairs with numerous doors, Meg noted, but without having seen the outside very well in the dark, she found it difficult to make out just how big the house might be. She wondered how many people lived there.

Catherine directed them to the room at one end of the hall where Lizzie would be sleeping. As her daughter went in and dropped her bags on one of the twin beds, Meg took a quick look around. Plain wooden furniture, a dresser and a night table with a Bible on it. The curtains, doubtlessly hand-sewn, were yellow-and-white-checked, and the beds had yellow sheets and unadorned white dust ruffles. There were no computer photos, posters, or decorations like Lizzie or her friends would have displayed. Instead, Meg saw that the room's inhabitant had hung up rows of notes, cards, and letters she must have received over the years.

The room where Will and Sam were to spend the night was very different. Meg saw free weights in one corner, an archery bow propped nearby, and posters of various athletes hung up on the walls. On the high chest of drawers, she spotted a framed photograph of several smiling Amish teenagers, buddies having a good time.

Sam reached for a quick good-night hug from

his mother, the fearful look in his eyes causing her to kneel down and put a hand on his cheek. She smiled at him. "We're right here," she murmured into his hair as she held him close, "and you'll be with your brother."

"Yeah, come on," Will said as he dropped his bags on the floor. "I'll tell you ghost stories."

Sam shot his mother a look of panic.

"Just kidding, Sam." Will laughed.

Meg hugged and reassured Sam for another minute before he was willing to let her go.

Catherine led Meg and James to the far end of the hall. The bedroom was spare, with two small windows framed by beige curtains, and furnished much like the others with a heavy wooden dresser and a night table in between twin beds. The beds looked freshly made.

"This is Annie's old room," Catherine explained. "She's married now and living next door. Amanda put clean sheets on while we were downstairs."

Meg and James tried to express their gratitude once again, but Catherine waved away their words. "We eat breakfast at six, but you don't need to get up that early. Is eight o'clock all right for you?"

"That would be wonderful."

Catherine nodded and headed toward the stairs. Meg closed the door.

"This is quite the situation," James said, dropping down onto one of the beds to take off his shoes.

There was a tap on the door.

"I know we've gone back to 1742," Lizzie said with sarcastic sweetness, "but could you please wake me when it's the present again?"

Meg yanked open the door. "Not funny, Lizzie." She looked past her daughter to scan the hallway. "And please shush. They might hear you."

The girl rolled her eyes. "Relax, there's no one up here but us. I looked. But come on, Mom, we're in some kind of time warp. We're in *Little House on the Prairie*! Which, by the way, was on the bookcase downstairs! Are you kidding me? Please just get us out of here tomorrow first thing."

James looked up at her. "How should I do that, Liz?" he asked in annoyance. "Build a car with paper-towel tubes and duct tape?"

Lizzie's expression turned dark. "I don't care what we have to do, but I'm not staying here a minute more than I have to."

Meg kept her annoyance in check. "Go on back to your room. We should all get some rest."

"It's *nine-thirty!* Who goes to bed at nine-thirty?"

"Tonight," Meg replied, "we do. And remember to make your bed in the morning and clean up after yourself in the bathroom. We're guests, so let's behave like guests."

"It's weird up here, all deserted. Everything's so ugly."

"Good night, sweetheart." Meg gently closed the door.

"Sure, what do you care?" Lizzie's complaints grew fainter as she moved down the hall. "You're not sharing a room with someone who thinks this is the eighteenth century."

Meg felt she couldn't move another muscle. She found one of her nightgowns in her suitcase, slipped it on, and crawled under the covers, falling instantly into a deep sleep.

Waking up now, she was amazed that her body, which had felt tired but fine the night before, could be so stiff and sore.

She looked at James, asleep in the other bed, then reached for her watch on the night table. The slight movement made her feel as if every single muscle in her body were screaming in protest. It was seven-forty.

"James," she called out, slightly panicked, "wake up! We're supposed to be downstairs at eight. That's in twenty minutes!"

He mumbled something and rolled away from her voice. With a long groan, Meg forced herself to sit up.

"You have to get up," she said with more force as she made her way to her purse for the small bottle of ibuprofen she always kept there. She was particularly sore on her side, where James had collided with her at the moment of impact.

"Oh, wow, everything aches." James stared at the ceiling, tentatively stretching out his arms.

"Here, you want two of these?" She held out the bottle. Whatever their problems were, for now she would have to put aside her resentment toward James to get through the situation. "We have to wake the kids up. I'm sure they're dead asleep, and we're supposed to have breakfast now."

Grumbling, the children threw on their clothes and headed downstairs, Lizzie still limping slightly. By the time they had all assembled in the kitchen, it was nearly eight-thirty. Meg saw that Sam had a huge, angry-looking lump on his forehead, but he didn't say anything about it, so she didn't bring it up.

They found five places set for them at the table, including glasses filled with orange juice. There were several boxes of cereal, a plate with chocolate-chip cookies, doughnuts, and what appeared to be homemade zucchini bread, plus a bowl of strawberry preserves. Next to all of that were pitchers with milk and water. The room was dim, and Meg realized that the windows were the only source of light. Of course, she thought. No electricity, but it was daytime, so it wouldn't be necessary to light lamps or candles.

Meg looked around. "I have to say, this house is so clean, you could perform brain surgery on the floor of any room."

The Hobart children sat down at the table and glowered. Lizzie touched the flowered plastic place mat with distaste. "Gross."

"These aren't normal cereals," Will complained. "What is this, all generic?"

"They're the same as cornflakes and Cheerios," James answered.

"My bed was so hard, I might as well have slept on the floor. And if I hadn't had my own blanket, I would have frozen to death under that thin thing they had on the bed." Lizzie reached for a cookie.

Meg ignored her remarks. "Did you see their daughter?"

"I saw her at some point, but she woke me up by accident, and it was dark, so I don't know if it was when she came in or got up to leave." Lizzie grinned. "Maybe she was out until all hours. These people are party animals."

Will laughed and high-fived his sister.

The door opened, and Catherine Lutz came inside, her face flushed with the cold. Will and Lizzie immediately fell silent. Sam poured himself a bowl of cereal.

Catherine removed her black cape, talking cheerfully as she hung it on a hook. "Good morning. I thought you might need some more sleep, so I just put this out. I can make you some hot food now. Eggs and ham? Coffee?"

"No, thank you," James answered. "This is plenty. But coffee would be great."

David Lutz appeared behind his wife, wiping his feet on the doormat before he came in. "Ah, I'm in time to sit with you. How are you folks feeling today?"

"Like the doctor warned us," Meg said. "We're stiff, but it'll pass."

David sat down at the head of the table. "Would one of you like to say grace?"

Sam, who had been reaching for the milk pitcher, froze, then dropped his arm into his lap. Will's and Lizzie's eyes widened.

Meg had no idea what constituted grace for these people. She doubted James did, either, which he confirmed with the note of doubt in his voice. "Uh, thank you, but no. It's your house, so please, you go ahead."

David nodded. "Our Father, who art in Heaven . . ."

Oh, thought Meg with relief, it's the Lord's Prayer. What had she been expecting? She and James joined in, their children sitting silently, the two elder ones doing a poor job of hiding their pained expressions. The Lutzes, Meg saw, either didn't notice or were gracious enough to pretend they didn't.

"Where is everybody?" Will asked when they

had finished. He took a bite of a doughnut. "Are you the only people here?"

David smiled. "Oh, there are lots of people here. The younger children are at school. The older ones are doing chores. Some of our children are married and don't live here, but they'll be by at some point. They live in the houses nearby, so the grandchildren run in and out a lot, too. Be careful you don't trip on them."

"Whoa," said Lizzie in surprise before she caught herself.

Meg realized that her daughter had never been exposed to an extended family living so close to one another. They barely had relatives, much less ones that might run in and out a lot.

"You didn't get to meet Amanda yesterday," Catherine said to Lizzie, "but she's breaking up the ice in front of the barn, and she'll be in a little later."

Lizzie's forced smile matched the tone of her words. "That's great."

Catherine brought over a pot of coffee and poured cups for Meg and James. "It snowed a little during the night, but mostly there is ice now."

"When you're done with your coffee," David said to James, "we can find out the situation with your car. I'll take you over to the repair shop."

James looked grim. "We'd better find out what we're dealing with. Thanks."

Meg saw that her children had finished eating. "Kids, why don't you clear your plates, then run upstairs and make your beds?"

"Sure, you bet." Will jumped up with false cheerfulness.

Meg happened to catch James's eye. She saw he was no more pleased with their older children's behavior than she was.

Finally, David and James left, and Meg was alone with Catherine, helping to clean up.

"How many children do you have?" Meg asked, stacking dirty dishes in the sink. She tried to ignore the soreness that accompanied her every move.

"Nine," Catherine said.

"Nine children," Meg echoed in amazement.

"Two are married. You met Jonathan and Eli. There's Amanda, who's sixteen, and Benjamin, who's seventeen. The youngest are Aaron and Rachel. They're eleven and eight. They were visiting at my sister's house last night. And then there's my daughter Barbara. She's getting married next week." Catherine began washing the dishes.

"Really?" Meg asked in surprise. "Next week?"

"Yes. We're having family and friends from all over to celebrate." She gave a little grin. "And do lots and lots of eating. The lunch and evening supper will be across the road at Joseph's house. He is one of the married children I told you about. About three hundred people are coming."

Meg reached for the small towel that was resting near the dish rack. She tried to picture herself being as calm as this woman if she were having three hundred guests at her house in a week.

"How will you manage   " Meg hesitated, wanting to ask more, but fearful she would say something foolish.

"Everyone helps," Catherine said. "Lots of people cooking, serving food, cleaning up."

Meg dried a pitcher, feeling ignorant and nosy at the same time. She didn't ask any further questions, and Catherine finished the rest of the dishes without volunteering anything else. When she was done, she excused herself. "It's laundry day. I know you're not feeling well, so you rest."

"You know, Catherine, I really don't know what will happen with the car," Meg said. She paused, unsure what she wanted to say or ask.

It was obvious the car wasn't going to be ready to go anywhere today, but they had no place else to go. Maybe the Lutzes would take them to a motel or something. Meg dreaded the idea of the five of them cooped up in a motel room for an indefinite period. Not to mention the cost. Yet they couldn't impose on these people any further. For all Meg knew, they hated having non-Amish people in their house.

Catherine looked at her. Her eyes, Meg realized, were a pale blue. They crinkled at the edges as she gave Meg a warm smile. "You're welcome to stay here as long as you wish."

"I . . . We can't . . ."

"You can if you want," Catherine said simply, heading out through another door leading from the room.

Chapter 8

Having persuaded Catherine that she was indeed up to performing some sort of work, Meg sat on the couch next to a veritable mountain of towels. Catherine had brought them to her from an outside clothesline, and they were cold and rigid from the December air. Meg shook them out as best she could with her sore shoulders, then folded them into thirds and in half. She paid close attention to the task, wanting this minimal contribution to be done properly. These people clearly had very high standards, at least in housekeeping, and she didn't want anybody to have to redo her job, small as it might be.

Meg found it was a relief to become totally engrossed in the task. She didn't have to think about the fact that she and her family were stranded with virtually no money, or that their only form of transportation was a twisted wreck that might not even be fixable. Nor did she have to think about how furious she was at her husband, who had lied to her, basically stolen all the family's money only to throw it away, and

119

brought them to this point. She could also block out the vague but horrible image of what their immediate future would look like when they figured out how to get from here to her parents' house.

Shake, fold, smooth, put to the side. The graying, scratchy linens made her recall the white towels in the bathrooms of their house in Charlotte. Lots of detergent, bleach, fabric softener, and a hot dryer kept those enormous Egyptian-cotton bath towels fluffy and blindingly white. They held a sweet, lightly perfumed scent, noticeable only when she wrapped herself up in one, an especially cozy feeling after it had been resting on the electric towel rack, warming on a winter's morning. Meg picked up a towel from the pile and held it to her nose. No perfume, but she found that she liked its absence, the smell of fresh air somehow infused into the rough fabric, making her want to take a deep breath.

Bracing, she thought, but probably not so inspiring when you're dripping wet on a freezing morning.

The door opened, and Meg tensed as she saw the expression on James's face. His mouth was set in a way that told her the news was not going to be good.

"What happened?" she asked. "You've been gone for hours."

He unzipped his jacket. "The place they towed

it to suggested we might want to get to a shop that specializes in vintage cars. So we did that. But the guy there can't even do anything until the insurance guys take a look. Someone will come by today or tomorrow, hopefully. They'll call us at the phone outside here, or I'll have to keep calling them."

"Is it a big deal to fix?"

"The guy gave it a quick look while I was there. He said there's extensive damage from the front fender all the way to the rear quarter panel. In other words, lots of bodywork needed on the driver's side."

"How long will that take?"

James scowled. "That's the thing. He said a week or two."

"A week or two?" Meg repeated. "We can't stay here for that long."

James gave her an exasperated look. "What would you have me do, Meg? You sound like Lizzie. I can't snap my fingers and get us out of here. If you have any ideas, please feel free to share them with me."

They were interrupted by Sam, who had been outside with his sister and brother. Meg had told them all to go for a walk earlier when their whining about how bored they were had become too much for her.

"Hey, sport, what are you up to?" James asked Sam.

"They were fighting too much. Besides, I'm freezing."

"Come over here." Meg moved the folded towels away and patted the couch beside her. "I'll warm you up."

Sam sat down, and she put her arms around him, vigorously rubbing his back through his fleece jacket. She kissed the top of his head as he leaned in to her. James went over to the sink to get himself a glass of water. Meg guessed he felt as uncomfortable as she did prying into their hosts' cupboards or refrigerator.

One of the doors opened, and the three of them looked up at the sound. An elderly man, slightly stooped, stood in the doorway. His hair was nearly white, and he had bangs falling across his forehead, plus a long, full beard. He was dressed just like all the other men they had seen in the house, in black pants with suspenders and a dark blue shirt. He wore a black vest as well.

"Ah," he said, smiling. "Our visitors." He came forward, moving to take a seat at the big table. "I am Samuel Lutz. David is my son." He jerked a thumb in the direction of the door from which he had emerged. "We live there."

James went over to introduce himself and Meg and shake Samuel's hand. Then Samuel turned his attention to Sam. "And who is this young man?"

Shyly, Sam identified himself.

Samuel Lutz's eyes lit up. "Ahh, another Samuel! Very good!"

Sam obviously hadn't put his name together with the name of this odd-looking man. "Oh. Yeah."

The older man smiled. "We will be good friends, then. I will call you Young Samuel."

Sam looked uncomfortable but said nothing.

"I heard we had visitors. I wanted to meet you before the crowd comes in for lunch. My daughter-in-law will be here soon, I think, to put it out."

As if on cue, Catherine joined them from outside. She was in conversation with a young girl dressed much like she was, down to the white head covering with the untied strings.

"Hello," said Catherine. "This is my daughter Amanda. She and your daughter are in one bedroom."

"Oh, yes." Meg looked at the girl with interest. "Lizzie said she didn't get a chance to meet you last night."

"I was out," Amanda answered with the family's accent, "but I got up early, so we never talked."

"But now it is lunch, so you'll meet her." Catherine moved to the kitchen area and opened the oven door to check on what she had inside. "Everyone will meet everyone."

Amanda pulled open a kitchen drawer.

"Thirteen," Catherine said. "Plus some little ones. Maybe three."

Amanda nodded and reached into the drawer to pull out flatware.

Meg whispered to Sam, "Run outside and get your sister and brother. We all need to help."

By the time the table had been set and everyone was assembled, there were seventeen people. They all seemed to be speaking in a language that sounded like German, although Meg couldn't be sure. As soon as they saw the Hobarts, they switched to English.

The Lutz family said grace silently, and Meg realized the spoken grace when they first arrived probably had been done for their benefit. Introductions were swift, and she didn't remember all of the names. A few stood out. The older man, Samuel Lutz, was married to Leah. Somewhat stout, with a full face and lips, she was polite but no more than that, lacking her husband's genuine warmth. Two men arrived with small children in tow, and Catherine explained that their wives were baking. Meg had no idea why that meant they had to miss lunch, but it didn't seem like the right moment to ask. She knew she would remember Barbara, a bubbly young woman who was introduced as the daughter getting married the following week. Jonathan, the older of the two sons who had helped them the night before, also joined them at the last minute.

Meg's children, silent with the strangeness of it all, seemed taken aback by the size of this lunchtime gathering, which apparently was a daily occurrence. Catherine indicated that the two teenage roommates should sit next to each other, and Amanda greeted Lizzie with a smile and obvious interest. Lizzie barely returned her greeting and said nothing more to her. The men and women took their places on opposite sides of the table.

With Meg and a stone-faced Lizzie joining them, the women helped serve what seemed like an endless succession of overflowing bowls and platters. The main meal consisted of bean soup, chicken in gravy, meat loaf, buttered noodles, brussels sprouts, peas and carrots, creamed corn, and hot biscuits with butter. The Hobart children ate little, pushing the food around on their plates, until they got to the desserts, which included pound cake, apple dumplings, rice pudding, and mixed fruit.

There was little conversation at the table. Meg observed the line of men across from her, all with the same haircut. The older ones had beards and no mustaches. Their clothing was virtually identical. The women kept their hair tucked under bonnets, and all had on the same simple dresses, some with black coverings like full aprons, the top half of which resembled an upside-down triangle. The dresses differed only in color: muted, dark tones of blue or purple or gray. Meg wondered at the fact that even by this point in the day their clothes remained perfectly pressed. She noted that the garments were held closed with straight pins rather than buttons or zippers. There was not a single piece of jewelry or a hint of makeup on any of them.

The men reported to one another on the progress of whatever they had been working on that morning. David had missed much of his morning work by taking James to see about the car, but he managed to get to the barn, where they were shoveling out manure, bringing it to an area where they stored it to be used as fertilizer. One of the men updated the others on repairs he was making on their horses' harnesses. James asked if he might help with that job, saying he didn't think he could manage a shovel just yet, but he could try to make himself useful until he could put his back into something. David nodded.

Lunch was over quickly. The men left, and the women cleaned up before dispersing. The smaller children were left behind, giving Meg an idea for something to occupy her own children's time. Catherine said it wasn't necessary for anyone to watch her grandchildren, that they would be fine playing near her, but Meg insisted that her children babysit. All three of them shot daggers at her with their eyes, but Meg was delighted to see that it wasn't long before they actually seemed to be enjoying interacting with the toddlers.

Amanda said a smiling goodbye to all of them and ran out to where her brother Jonathan waited in a buggy.

"She's off to deliver to the store, and I'm going to prepare for supper," Catherine explained, setting out a large knife and chopping board. "I have to get back out to hang up the rest of the laundry."

She hadn't even sat down after serving lunch, Meg observed, and now she was on to the next meal and more chores. Did she ever rest?

"Do you mind if I ask you what store you mean?" As she spoke, Meg saw an opportunity to repeat her earlier job of drying dishes and reached for the dish towel.

Catherine had begun cutting up potatoes to put into a large pot of water. "It is a store in town. King's is the name. We make them things to sell. Bread, cakes, jams. Different things, depending on the season. That's why my daughter Annie and my daughter-in-law Sue weren't at lunch. Today was their day to do the baking. They brought fresh bread and rolls in the morning, and now Amanda will take over the pies with Jonathan."

"You make everything here?"

Catherine nodded. "Oh, yes."

"Jams?"

"Jams, jelly, all kinds of preserves. We pickle things. Make vinegars, too."

Meg was fascinated. "I'd love to see how you do that."

Catherine heaved the large pot onto the stove and covered it. "We make a lot of it in the warmer months. I will take you downstairs, and you can see it. After I finish cutting up some vegetables, I'll show you."

"Thank you." Meg's admiration for this busy woman was growing. "I've always loved the idea of making jams and preserves, but I never had time to learn." She regretted the words the second they had left her mouth. To say she didn't have enough time to someone who worked as hard as Catherine was ludicrous. "I guess," she amended, "I didn't make the time."

Catherine was immersed in cutting up carrots and celery and didn't reply. When she finished, she set down her knife. "I will take you downstairs."

Meg followed her to a door that led to the basement steps. As she reached the bottom of the staircase, she caught her breath at the sight before her. Although the room was primarily below ground level, windows had been installed high up enough to let outside daylight in. Like everything else in the house, the basement was spotless. What surprised Meg were the rows upon rows of open wooden shelving, set up like library stacks. The shelves sagged under the weight of hundreds of glass bottles and jars containing a vast array of different foods. Nearby, Meg saw a table with what appeared to be a setup for the final packaging, with squares of fabrics, rubber bands, labels, colored markers, and scissors.

"You do all this yourself?" she asked in disbelief.

"Oh, no. All the women in the family do it. The women and the girls. We have much more in my daughter's and son's houses."

Catherine waited patiently while Meg walked up and down a few of the rows. She marveled at the intricacy of this business, at the fact that it was tucked into such a tiny space. The shelves had handwritten labels identifying the containers' contents. Onion Relish, Apple Jam, Apricot Chutney, Chowchow, Strawberry Preserves, Chili Oil, Sweet Pickled Peppers, Bread-and-Butter Pickles, Corn Relish, Rosemary Vinegar. Meg was struck by the beauty of all the bottle shapes and the colors and textures of the foods within them. "Amazing. Such variety, too. What a job all this must be," she exclaimed.

"It's not hard once you learn how," Catherine replied. "Now I must get back to cooking."

Turning to go, Meg caught sight of a large area at the far side of the basement devoted to storing what she saw were root vegetables. She could identify onions, carrots, parsnips, potatoes, and something she guessed was horseradish in large crocks lined up in neat rows.

When they rejoined the children in the living room, they found that Samuel Lutz had returned, this time with a puppy in his arms. The elderly man was seated on the couch, talking to his great-grandchildren as he stroked the puppy's head. They must have been used to the dog, Meg thought, because they weren't exclaiming over it the way children typically did at such a sight. Now that she thought about it, she realized she had passed a number of dog bowls set out near the back entrance to the house. Some of the barking she had heard coming from outside must have come from dogs belonging to the Lutzes.

Will didn't seem interested in the scene before him. He sat at one of the folding tables, flipping through the pages of a book. Lizzie, however, was scratching the puppy under its chin, making cooing sounds, and Sam was sitting next to the older man, staring at the light brown ball of fur.

Samuel Lutz must have noticed the boy's interest. He held the puppy out to him. "Young Samuel?"

Sam's face lit up as he reached for the dog and nestled him in his lap. He looked happier than Meg had seen him in weeks. She watched him rub his cheek against the dog's soft head, the widest smile on his face. Of course, Meg thought. I can't believe I didn't I think of it before. Sam should have a dog. It was a simple and wonderful idea.

Her heart sank as she remembered that they were heading to her parents', who had never wanted anything to do with a pet in their house. As a child, Meg had begged them to let her have a dog or a cat, anything at all, but they always said no. Pets were messy. There were cages and bowls to clean and expensive food to buy. Meg felt pretty certain they were unlikely to have softened on the topic as they had gotten older.

She sighed, watching the puppy lick Sam's face, her son giggling with pleasure. Samuel Lutz leaned over and spoke quietly to him about the dog, lifting a paw and showing him the pads underneath, gently opening the dog's mouth to explain about the teeth.

Meg went over to a window and looked out. She wished she were in a position to do something so good for Sam. She looked at the clothesline where Catherine had hung out the wet clothes. The different-colored dresses and the men's shirts, black pants, and jackets were attached with clothespins in neat lines, each type of garment grouped, each garment attached at the same points. It looked to her like a line of people—flat people, to be sure, but a big family, ordered and serene.

With a start, she realized she had been so preoccupied, she hadn't yet gone outside to look around. "I'm going to take a walk unless anyone needs me," she announced to the room in general.

"Can I come?" Will asked, reaching for his jacket, which he had thrown on a chair.

Meg was surprised. "Of course, honey. Let me grab my coat." She hurried upstairs, feeling the soreness in her back. As she passed the room Will and Sam were occupying, she paused long enough to notice that, while their beds could technically be considered made, it would have been easy to think otherwise. She hurried to get her jacket, anxious to get out.

With her son beside her, Meg stepped out into the cold daylight to see that the house was set amid enormous open fields. The ground sloped beneath the gray sky, providing a panoramic view of other farms, their neat houses and barns nestled close to tall pairs of silos and pens. Straight paved roads crisscrossed the landscape. The bare tree branches and frozen ground gave the scene a stark silence. Off in the distance, she saw a horse and buggy on the road, the horse trotting at a brisk clip.

"Like a painting," Meg murmured.

"This place is *so* weird" was Will's response.

She turned to him. "You know, you guys are being pretty horrible to the kids here."

"Oh, please." He gave a little snort of disgust. "These kids are the biggest bunch of losers I've ever seen."

"Why? Because they're different from you?"

"Because they're different from *humans.* The stuff they wear! And the way they talk. It's like we're in some bad museum exhibit or something."

Meg shook her head. "I guess I'm surprised at you. I would have expected you to be a little more curious about something so different from what you've always known. Not so judgmental."

"Don't try to guilt me with that 'I'm disappointed in you' stuff," Will said. "This is just plain wacko."

Meg frowned. She tried to remember if she and James had ever actively tried to instill any curiosity in Will about the way other people lived. Over the years, the family had vacationed at Disney World and the Grand Canyon, in the Caribbean and the Outer Banks. Fun places, and beautiful, but hardly educational when it came to learning about the rest of the world. Their dinner-table conversation had focused on the kids' daily activities and who needed to get what or go where.

She shoved her hands in her coat pockets. "Let's walk."

Meg saw now that the Lutzes' house was quite large, with a fresh-looking coat of white paint and dark-green shades at all the first-floor windows. Two rocking chairs and small outdoor tables sat to one side of the front porch. On a side porch, she noted used children's toys, a dented tricycle, and an assortment of mismatched chairs, one of which held a sleeping gray cat. Empty terra-cotta and hanging pots suggested the display of numerous plants and flowers in the warmer weather. Meg noticed several birdhouses filled with birdseed. She was surprised to discover that what she assumed was a portion of the house was a second, attached house, slightly smaller but similar in design. That, she realized, must be where Samuel and Leah Lutz lived, and the doorway through which he had emerged when they first met must be the connection.

Meg came upon a patch of land that was clearly a garden, now put to bed for the winter. With her son behind her, she walked along its borders.

"Mom? What's going to happen to us?"

She stopped, startled by her son's unexpected question, by the fear in his tone. She had been wondering when the children would start to ask more pointed questions about their situation. Apparently the moment was now. She decided to see how far into it Will really wished to go.

"What'll happen is we'll get the car repaired, and we'll head up to Grandma and Grandpa's."

She waited to see if that explanation would hold him. No such luck.

"That's not what I mean, and you know it. Stop treating me like a little kid," he said.

She turned to face him. "Okay, Will. Here's the truth: We're kinda starting over. We'll be okay. But for now we're pretty much broke, and that's for real. I'm not sure if you guys really get that, but if you don't, you will soon."

"Yeah, in a way, I still don't believe it."

"I know," Meg said. "Sometimes I don't, either. But we have to stay with your grandparents because we need to find work and save money. Then we'll take it from there."

He closed his eyes and made a pained face. "It's gonna be so *awful* to live with them. They don't even like us."

Meg wanted to agree with him but knew she shouldn't. "It'll be okay, Will. We'll work it out."

"How do you work out people not wanting you around?"

"You don't know they feel that way—"

"Mom." Will gave her a look that told her to stop placating him.

Meg reached out to straighten the collar of his fleece jacket, automatically registering that he needed a haircut. "Here's the story. I'm going to work as hard and as fast as I can to figure out something that will allow us to be independent again. That I promise."

"What about you and Dad? You guys seem really angry at each other. Like, more angry than I've ever seen you. Are you getting divorced?"

She gazed into Will's eyes and saw he was not

going to let her get away with anything less than the truth. He might be her little boy, but he was growing up fast. She took a breath. "I don't know," she said. "I just don't know."

He looked away.

"I'm sorry, honey," she said.

He nodded, then walked off without another word. She watched him go. The wind picked up, whipping his sandy hair in every direction.

She pulled her collar more tightly around her neck and was still staring after him when she heard James come up behind her. "Everything okay?" he asked.

"As okay as possible, I suppose," she replied without turning around.

He rested his hands on her shoulders. Startled, she slipped out of his grasp. "What are you doing?"

He shrugged. "Just trying to be nice. I mean, here we are, so we might as well make the best of things. No point in being angry, is there?"

"There is a point, yes, there is. Being here doesn't mean you get a free pass. Nothing has changed."

"Come on, Meg," he said, annoyed. "You can't keep rehashing the past. We have to move forward."

"We haven't exactly 'rehashed the past.' We haven't even talked about it. Besides, you may not be happy with what happens when we move forward. Let me put it this way: I don't know if there *is* a forward for us."

"You're not still thinking of breaking up the family, are you? That would be crazy."

"Wow." Meg shook her head in disbelief. "You actually think that letting a little time go by should be enough to wipe the slate clean. I should just forgive and forget. That would be the most convenient thing for everybody."

"What's wrong with forgiving?"

"Can you even forgive a person who's not sorry?"

"I *am* sorry. Don't you think I feel—"

David Lutz came around the corner of the house, wearing muddied black rubber boots and holding a bucket in one hand. At the sight of him, James stopped talking.

"I'm going to the barn. Want to come?" David asked.

Relieved to have this argument interrupted, Meg nodded and strode toward him, James right behind her. The barn was a huge building set away from the main house. The smell of horses grew stronger as they approached. Inside, they saw shovels, pitchforks, rakes, an ax, and other tools hanging from hooks on the walls. The roof extended up two stories, with ladders and steps leading to haylofts and other perches. The wooden floor was swept completely clean.

"Horses are this way," David said, going down

a passageway to the left. He pointed to a large cobweb in a corner. "My website."

Startled by the unexpected joke, Meg and James both laughed. Meg knew that their hosts were people like everyone else, but David's comment made her realize that she hadn't quite believed it until now. They weren't saints or judges. They knew what was going on in the world, they could joke about it, they had a sense of humor. And they weren't going to be offended by questions or mistakes. For the first time since they had arrived, Meg felt herself relax.

Coming around a corner, she saw two large stalls with five horses, several of them munching on hay. David walked up to the nearest horse and stroked his neck. "Most are for farming, but we keep two just for pulling the buggies."

James put out an open palm under another horse's muzzle. "Beautiful animals."

"They're like family to us, you know." David moved past the horses. "Over here, you can see where we keep the buggies."

They followed him into a partitioned area housing two buggies, with space for a third. They were identical from the back, gray with gray coverings and high, narrow wheels, plus a variety of red triangles and lights on the back to render them more visible at night. Meg looked into the front seat of one, surprised to see the woodwork on what was the equivalent of a dashboard. The rich dark wood was intricately carved and polished until it gleamed. It had been too dark the night before to notice.

David indicated the empty space. "The one that goes there belongs to my son Jonathan. He got his own when he turned sixteen."

"No heating, I guess. Cold in the winter, riding in these," James observed.

David smiled. "We use armstrong heaters. You know those?"

James shook his head. "No, I don't."

David threw an arm around James's shoulders and pulled him tight. "This is an armstrong heater."

James grinned. "Oh. Got it."

Laughing, David led them outside. He pointed to the fields stretching out before them. "We grow lots of crops. Tomatoes and peas, which we sell. Hay for feeding. Catherine has a garden with herbs and about, oh, twenty vegetables. We pickle and can them, some for us and some to sell."

Meg nodded. "Catherine showed me."

"In the spring, we have a road stand. Tourists buy vegetables into the early fall. Also, we have chickens, so we sell their eggs." David pointed to a white house across the road, then to another one some fifty yards away. "That is where my son and daughter live, those two houses. They have the cows. For dairy."

The tour was interrupted by the appearance of a boy and a girl running up to where the trio of adults stood, only to come to a stop before them. They were both blond, with pale-blue eyes, and they regarded Meg and James with open curiosity. The little boy had on the same type of wide-brim hat the men wore, while the little girl was bareheaded, her fine blond hair neatly pulled away from her face.

"These are my children, home from school," David said. "My son Aaron and my daughter Rachel."

"Hello," James said, smiling at them.

Meg took a step closer. "Hi. I guess you were at school this morning when we got up, so we didn't get to see you then."

They both nodded and continued gazing at her, their expressions friendly and direct.

"How old are you?" James asked.

"I am eleven," Aaron answered. "My sister is eight years."

"It's very nice to meet you," Meg said. Rachel gave her a wide grin. "Did you meet our children? They're inside," Meg went on.

The idea of other children clearly sounded exciting to them.

"May we go? Please?" Rachel asked her father.

"Yes, but after you say hello, you do your chores. Fun is later."

They ran off, smiling.

Dinner that night was served at five o'clock to an even larger crowd than at lunch. With the exception of Benjamin, the son who was away, all the Lutz children were at the table. Meg was able to straighten out who were the two married ones: Joseph, the son who lived across the road with his wife, Sue, and their two children, and Annie, the daughter who lived in the house immediately next door with her husband, Nicholas, and their three children. All their children were under the age of five, and they were quiet throughout the meal, other than a few requests for assistance. The few who were old enough to comprehend that the Hobarts were outsiders stared at them with fascination.

After grace, all of them worked their way through fried chicken, ham with pineapple rings, rice, butternut squash, beets, and sauerkraut. Taking a bite of corn bread, Meg reminded herself that, unlike her, these people performed physical labor all day long, so they could handle the calories they were consuming at meals. It also dawned on her that James must be unhappy with what they were being served. He had always been far stricter than she when it came to his diet. Just looking at the fat and cholesterol on his plate was probably enough to give him a heart attack. Normally, she thought, she would have been trying to figure out how she could find him something he would prefer to eat without hurting her hostess's feelings. At the moment, however, she wasn't concerned with his preferences.

What she was concerned with were her older children. Yet again, their behavior was making her want to wring their necks. Will refused to make eye contact with anyone at the table despite the obvious desire of Eli Lutz, the fourteen-year-old son who had helped them the previous night, to talk to him. Eli kept glancing over at him but seemed to know better than to initiate anything. Lizzie appeared to be barely enduring Amanda's efforts to converse with her. Meg was surprised by Amanda's persistent attempts to be friendly despite Lizzie's continued rudeness.

With relief, Meg saw that Sam was deep in conversation with Aaron, the eleven-year-old Meg had met outside the barn. From across the table, where she sat with the women, eight-year-old Rachel watched the two boys with unwavering intensity.

Here's what's wrong with this picture, Meg said to herself: As a child gets older, his or her manners should get better, not worse. It was only her youngest child who displayed any manners at all. The older ones were clearly on the decline when it came to even minimal politeness. What I thought of as typical teenage behavior, Meg rebuked herself, may have been typical or not—but that didn't make it right.

As they were finishing dessert, Amanda, Eli,

Aaron, and Rachel stood up in a row facing the table, joined by Annie Lutz's five-year-old. Hands at their sides, with no musical accompaniment, they began to sing. Meg didn't catch all the words, but she understood that it was a song primarily about gratitude. All the diners were silent, watching and listening, smiles on their faces. Old Samuel nodded in time. Even his wife, the unsmiling Leah, seemed pleased.

Meg was mesmerized by their sweet, pure voices. More startling to her was that they showed no signs of embarrassment or resentment at being forced to perform. Their faces registered only concentration on their task. Meg saw that her own children could hardly bear to listen to the performance. They looked as if they would give years of their life to be anywhere else. Even Sam squirmed uncomfortably.

When the children were finished singing, the two eldest sat down and the other three remained standing to sing a second song. Meg noticed that the five-year-old didn't know all the words, but that didn't stop him from participating as best he could. Next, David and Catherine Lutz sang together. Afterward, no one applauded. Almost everyone seemed to have enjoyed it all, but no comments were made. Meg's children rolled their eyes at one another. Dinner was concluded.

Meg tried to imagine the children of anyone she knew getting up and singing so gracefully and willingly. Impossible. Why, she wondered, was it so outlandish to think that children could get up and sing without imitating rock stars or rappers, without trying to appear cool or amused by the irony of their own performance? Some kids would play the piano for their parents' friends, and she could recall seeing girls perform a dance they had made up or planned to do for something at school. That kind of thing, yes, she thought; and always followed by extravagant praise. This was entirely different. It was a simple and somehow *vulnerable* performance. Traditional. Something that spoke of beliefs and prayers passed down from one generation to another. And so very beautiful.

Serving the evening meal, Meg saw, was far from the end of the day's work for the women in the house. When the kitchen area was spotless, Catherine and her daughters began sewing. They had a pile of men's black pants and jackets on the table and were repairing torn seams, replacing hooks and eyes, letting down hems. Amanda was stitching together pieces of black cloth.

"Amanda, are you making an apron?" Meg asked, taking a sip of coffee.

The girl looked up at her. "Yes."

"We make our clothes," Catherine explained. "Everything for the women and the children. Some families make their men's summer hats as well, the straw ones, but we don't do that. We buy those."

Meg tried to tally up what it would mean to make or repair the wardrobe for a family of eleven. A wardrobe limited in style, to be sure, but a huge number of garments that required skill and precision, since they had to look a very specific way.

"I use a sewing machine, mostly," Amanda added, "but I will not have time to do much tonight, so I am just working on it a little bit."

Catherine could see the question forming in Meg's mind. "It's not electric. A treadle sewing machine. It was my mother's."

"Mom, look!"

Meg turned to see Sam coming toward her, the puppy trotting along behind him.

"He's following me," Sam cried happily. "He knows me!"

Catherine stood up and went to a kitchen cabinet. "Maybe you want to give him a treat."

Sam took the piece of cracker Catherine handed him. "Here, Rufus. Here, boy."

As Sam held the puppy close and fed it the small treat, the dog licked his face. Meg had never seen Sam look so blissful.

Which made her think of her other two children.

"Would you please excuse me?" Meg rose from the table. She found Lizzie and Will upstairs, sprawled out on the beds in Amanda's room. Will was lying on his back, tossing a ball up in the air and catching it.

Her daughter sat up as soon as Meg entered the room. "Mom, thank goodness. Can you tell us what's going on? When are we getting out of here?"

"I don't know any more now than I did before. We have to see what happens with the car."

"We could take a plane. Why do we have to wait for the stupid car? It's horrible, anyway. Driving in that little car is, like, the worst thing in the world."

"Is that so?" Meg made no effort to hide her lack of sympathy. " 'The worst thing in the world.' That's really saying something."

Will raised himself up on one arm. "Come on, Mom. This place is a loony bin. You gotta do something."

Meg looked from one to the other. "How about we do this: You two stop behaving like spoiled brats. For however long we're here, you smile and act grateful for any little thing anyone does for you. I don't care if you *are* grateful, but *act* grateful. Ask how you can help anytime you're not occupied. And then actually help."

"That's not fair! We cleared the dishes when you—" Lizzie burst out.

"No, now you don't speak. You only listen," Meg interrupted sharply. "I don't think you two understand how upset I am with you. I can't believe how awful you're being to the kids here. They want to talk to you. Talk to them!"

Will groaned. "They're so lame."

"It's you and your sister who are 'so lame,' Will." Meg didn't raise her voice, but her anger was escalating. "I don't see why these people are willing to put up with two sulky, self-absorbed teenagers when they don't have to. But that's going to stop." Meg paused, then pointed to the bed Lizzie was on, the covers carelessly yanked up. "Whatever you do, please do it properly. These people keep their house a certain way. I won't have you creating any additional work for them. They work hard enough." She looked at her son. "That goes for you, too."

"Take it easy, already," Lizzie said. "We get it. You want us to become Amish."

Meg's eyes flared. "It would be a massive improvement over what you seem to have become. I don't want you to become Amish. I want you to become people. Nice people."

"Okay, Mom." Will sounded a conciliatory note. "I'll try."

"Good," Meg said sharply. "Lizzie?"

"All right, all right. We're stuck here, so fine." Lizzie's voice turned exaggeratedly sweet. "I'll be a perfect lady."

Meg matched her tone to her daughter's. "That would be lovely, dear."

The three of them looked at one another in a tense detente. Then, with a quick sigh, Meg leaned down to kiss them good night. "I understand this isn't easy, kids," she said, smoothing back Lizzie's hair. "But I'd like to see you rise to the occasion. I know you can do it."

Wan smiles followed her as she turned to leave the room. She headed down the dark hall to the bedroom she shared with James, not eager to get into another argument.

She felt as if she had been dropped into a different world, one in which everything was inside out—especially her family. Overall, she decided, this had been one of the longest and strangest days she could ever remember.

Chapter 9

Aside from the buggy's constant bouncing, it was remarkably cozy in the back, Meg thought, adjusting the blanket on her lap. The temperature may have been low, but the sun poked through the clouds, making the day feel warmer. Plastic windows acted as a windshield and gave some protection from the elements. While David Lutz and James rode up front, Meg was content to sit behind them, looking out onto the passing farms. There were still patches of ice and snow glistening in the fields and along the road. She could hear bits and pieces of the men's conversation, which seemed to be about crop rotation, but made no effort to follow it.

As much as she liked the Lutzes, Meg hoped that when they reached the garage, the car would be miraculously fixed and ready to go. Staying a couple of nights was one thing; freeloading for an extended period was another. She was too embarrassed to admit to their hosts that they couldn't afford to stay anywhere else. If luck was with them, they could pack up the kids, say thank you to the Lutzes, and leave the farm without burdening them further.

The buggy left the quiet country roads and traveled on bigger, busier routes. Meg was amazed that the cars and trucks passing within what seemed like inches didn't hit them. Just as she was beginning to feel her stomach had been jogged up and down past the point of discomfort, they turned in to the repair shop, its sign announcing that it specialized in vintage cars. Let's hope so, she thought, tossing aside the blanket and getting out. James joined her, but David stayed behind, saying he would wait for them.

A middle-aged man in stained gray work clothes emerged from the back of the shop, recognizing James at once from their earlier meeting.

"Ah, the '69 Mustang," he said, extending his hand. "I've been expecting you." He turned to Meg. "We had a long talk, your husband and I. Beautiful car."

"Okay, Ray," said James. "Lay it on me."

"It's not as bad as it could be, but it's definitely not good. Driver's side is a mess. So you're talking about all new metal, headlight, front fender, paint job—I'm going to do my best to blend the paint so we don't have to repaint the whole car."

"How long will all this take?" Meg asked.

He shrugged. "Like I told your husband, I

think you're probably looking at a week or two."

"Oh, no," she breathed.

"Listen," James said, "we're really in a bind here. Isn't there any way we can make this happen in less time?"

"I'll do the best I can for you, but I wouldn't bet on it. This is pretty time-consuming, and what with the paint and all . . ."

"Yeah, I understand." James was visibly frustrated, but it was clear there was no one to blame.

"You still at that phone number you gave me?"

James nodded. "I'll call you tomorrow anyway. We're at an Amish house, so there's no phone inside. It's easy to miss a call."

"Right." Ray held out his hand again. "Sorry the news isn't better. Look on the bright side. The car will be fine in the end. And at least insurance is willing to pay to fix it. I'll go get you the paperwork." He disappeared into the recesses of the shop.

"A week!" Meg repeated. "How can we stay here for that long?"

James cursed under his breath. "I told David that we wanted to pay him if we had to stay any longer. He said in no uncertain terms they wouldn't take any money from us."

"It isn't right for us to use them like some kind of hotel."

"I know, I know. I feel awful about it."

Taking the computer printout from Ray, they thanked him and left. As they approached the buggy, James leaned over to whisper to Meg. "We're going to have to get them to take us to a motel or something."

"Which we can't afford," she replied.

David was sitting in the buggy. He looked up at James. "How is your car?"

"Not great. It's going to be a while. At least a week."

"A week?" David readied the reins. "Excellent. We shall have the pleasure of your company for a little bit longer."

James began to protest. "No, David, please listen—"

David grinned. "We still have so much to learn from you English. Your ways are so interesting and unusual."

Meg laughed as she replaced the blanket on her lap. "We're just a tourist attraction to you, eh?"

He turned to face her, more serious. "We were both on that road the other night. This is how it should be. No need to talk about it more."

He made a clicking sound, and the horse began to trot. At Meg's request, he stopped at a super-market so she could run inside. She was out of ibuprofen, which she and James still needed, and she wanted to get some cleaning supplies. If her family was going to be staying in the house, she decided, she could at least take responsibility for the quarters upstairs. It occurred to her that she would have to call her parents to inform them of the delay, but she pushed it out of her head. She didn't feel like dealing with it at the moment.

Carrying her grocery bags back to the house, she saw Barbara, the soon-to-be-married daughter, sweeping off the front porch. A brown-and-black dog kept watch by her side. Meg smiled. "Good morning."

"Good morning to you." Barbara returned the smile.

Meg glanced down at the dog, who was eyeing her warily. "I don't believe I've seen him. Or is it a her?"

"Oh, this is Racer."

"Because he's fast?"

"He used to be, but that was a long time ago."

Meg knelt, setting down a bag, and let him sniff her hand.

Barbara went on, "Your son Samuel really likes him. Racer spent a lot of time with him this morning."

Meg looked up at her. "He does love your dogs here. Do you happen to know where Sam is now?"

"He and your other son went with Eli to work in the barn."

"Really?" Meg was happy, if surprised, to hear

that her boys were out of the house, doing something useful.

"If you are looking for your daughter, she went with my mother to Annie's." Barbara nodded in the direction of the house next door. "They're baking. For the store."

Lizzie was baking with the women? Wonders never cease, Meg thought. She grabbed her grocery bag and stood up. "Thank you, Barbara. Do you think it would be all right if I went to Annie's?"

"Oh, yes." The young woman resumed her sweeping. "I will go there soon, too."

Meg went inside to unpack the grocery bags before walking over to Annie's house. Like the Lutzes', it was painted white and had dark-green window shades behind all the first-floor windows. Meg had noticed those same green shades in a number of the houses during her buggy ride, so she guessed it wasn't a coincidence.

When she was almost there, a side door opened, and Lizzie emerged. As soon as she saw her mother approaching, she hurried over, still limping slightly on her bruised foot. "I thought I'd never get out of there!" she burst out in greeting. "Catherine said I should go with her, and I couldn't find a way to say no." She gave Meg a look. "Because now I'm such a perfect lady."

"Ahh, yes," Meg said.

"Yeah, well, they have some kind of insane assembly line going on in there." She shuddered. "These people give me the willies."

Meg sighed. She should have known it was too good to be true. "Okay, listen. If you're going back, please clean up in the bathroom we've been using. I have a sponge and stuff in the cabinet beneath the sink. Straighten the towels, wipe down the sink and toilet, all that stuff."

"Oh, ew—*no*."

Meg regarded her with impatience. "I'm not asking you, Lizzie. I'm telling you." She moved past her daughter.

"Wait," Lizzie yelled after a moment. "What about the car?"

"It could be another week," Meg replied over her shoulder. She was glad she was already a few yards away so she didn't have to respond to her daughter's wail.

"WHAT? A *week? No* WAY!"

Meg knocked on the door, glancing back to see Lizzie frozen to the same spot, staring at her. "Ice your foot, honey," she called out, flashing her daughter a bright smile before a voice hastened her inside.

The first thing to strike Meg was the warmth of the kitchen and the incredible aroma of apples and cinnamon. The room was a scene of vivid color and motion, the women in their bonnets, dressed in deep-hued tones of teal, green, purple, and blue, all moving smoothly and efficiently from one task to another. They were quiet, immersed in their jobs, although they looked up to murmur a greeting to their visitor.

"Hello, Meg." Catherine welcomed her with a smile. "You are doing well today so far?"

"Thank you, I'm fine."

Meg watched in fascination, noting row upon row of uncooked pie crusts in aluminum pie plates set up along an enormous table. She saw that the kitchen had a huge kitchen island and two large double ovens, all four of which were already pressed into service baking batches of the fragrant pies. Catherine and her mother-in-law, Leah, were rolling out additional pie dough on large floured wooden boards. Sue, who was married to Joseph, the eldest Lutz son, and lived across the street, and Amanda held large ceramic bowls and used wooden spoons to pour the apple filling into the crusts. Catherine and Leah moved behind them quickly to put the covering layers of dough on the fruit filling. Annie, whose house it was, followed right behind them, expertly pinching the edges to form perfectly scalloped ridges. Amanda then made X-shaped slits in the centers.

Meg hesitated but decided to jump in. "Is there some way I could help?"

Leah gave her a quizzical look, but Catherine

replied at once. "You need oven mitts. We will take the finished pies out in a minute."

With that, Meg was drawn into the whirlwind of the group, removing the golden-crusted pies from the hot oven and carefully handing them off to be whisked into a nearby room to cool before being wrapped for sale. When the ovens were empty, they refilled every rack and began preparing a third batch.

Meg marveled at the efficiency of the operation but even more so at the pleasure the women seemed to take in what they were doing. They obviously enjoyed one another's company, and rather than trudging through a task they must have done hundreds of times, they seemed to find it completely engaging. At one point Leah started to sing something that Meg guessed to be a hymn, and the others joined in. Meg found their voices soothing.

"Will you stop after the apple pies today?" she asked during a momentary lull in the activity.

"Barbara will come later, and we will make other pies," Annie answered. She adjusted her wire-rimmed glasses and smoothed her apron front. "Each week is different. Later this week, shoofly pie and whoopee pies. Every morning there is bread and muffins. Tomorrow, I think, we will make carrot cake, peanut butter cookies, and some pastries."

"Yum," Meg said.

Annie laughed. "Yes, but maybe not if you see them every day for years."

"Annie can resist them," Catherine said, smiling. "But we always make enough to have here as well."

"I'm sure." Meg grinned.

"We also bake for some restaurants and bakeries. We don't make so much now. In the warm months, there are many more tourists." Catherine washed her hands at the sink. "Now Amanda and I must go to make lunch. Jonathan will take her to the store with these pies later today."

"Would you mind if I went with them, just to see the store?" Meg asked.

"That would be fine." Putting on her wrap, Catherine turned to Amanda. "You finish up here and then come."

It was only a short distance back to the Lutz house, but Meg used the opportunity of being alone with Catherine to tell her about the delay with the car repairs. Catherine only nodded calmly. Somehow Meg felt she couldn't leave it at that; she owed this woman more of an explanation.

Meg stopped walking and put a hand on the other woman's arm to get her to stop as well. "Please understand. We don't want to take advantage of your generosity."

Catherine's blue eyes held her usual direct gaze. "You do not."

"We—my husband—he lost his job," Meg

managed to get out. "We're going to my parents in upstate New York because we pretty much have nothing. We have to stay there until we get back on our feet."

Catherine took this in, nodding, her expression unchanged.

"That's why we can't leave our car. If we weren't in this financial situation, we never would have stayed in your house like this. I mean, we're strangers. Five strangers, no less, and not even Amish. We know this is a huge imposition on your family."

Catherine smiled gently and put a hand over Meg's. "You are here, that's all there is to know. If there is anything we can do to help you, we want to do that."

Tears of relief stung Meg's eyes. She hadn't realized what a burden it had been, keeping the secret of why they were traveling and why they hadn't made plans to leave the Lutz household. She also couldn't remember the last time she had met such generous, good-hearted people. "Thank you," she whispered.

"Now," Catherine said, starting to move forward again, "we will have lunch. Today is a good day to take a little rest after."

Meg shook off her melancholy thoughts. "Ah, you *do* sometimes rest."

"Of course I do. But I meant *you* should take a rest today. I will be doing the ironing."

Meg hurried to keep up with the other woman's brisk pace. She imagined her old pink leather appointment book in Catherine's hands. Do everything in the whole world, it would say on each day's page. The image brought a smile to Meg's face.

It occurred to her that she had gone forty-eight hours without a scheduled appointment. I knew there was something really amiss, Meg thought wryly. The upheaval wasn't in her marriage or their financial ruin or being in a place that was unfamiliar in the truest sense of the word. It was that she didn't have her entire day scheduled down to the minute. No rushing around doing errands, no sense of juggling everyone's schedule.

It was, she decided, pretty great.

When they got into the house, Sam came running to greet her, hugging her around the waist. The bump on his head was turning dark shades of blue and purple, but he didn't seem to know it was even there.

"Mommy, where have you been?" He rushed on excitedly without waiting for an answer. "Aaron took me to collect eggs from the chickens before he left for school. It was so fun!" He took a step back, sharing his newfound expertise. "They don't lay as much in the cold weather, you know, but they do lay some eggs. I got two all by myself. At first I was scared, but then I wasn't!"

Meg grinned. "That is extremely cool, Sam."

"Aaron was really nice. He let me put out their feed and everything. They kind of smelled, but that was okay. And you know what? He said if you and Dad and his parents said it was okay, I could go to school with him one day. He goes to a special Amish school. All the grades in one room, first grade up to eighth grade. I hafta see this."

"It's fine with me if it's okay with everyone else."

Sam gave her another squeeze. "Thanks, Mom. You're the best." He turned to go. "I left Rufus in my bedroom, so I better get back."

Well, Meg thought, Sam was looking more relaxed than he had in ages, and he was obviously having the most fun of anyone in their family. Who would have guessed?

She caught a glimpse of Will and Eli walking past the window and went over to watch them. Her thirteen-year-old had his fleece jacket zipped up under his chin, his hands deep in his pockets. Eli wore the customary black brimmed hat and simple black jacket. He was talking and gesturing. Will nodded, his face neutral. Meg knew that face; it indicated he was participating in the conversation but didn't want anyone to think he actually cared about it. At least he was participating, she told herself. That was an improvement over yesterday.

Lunch was another huge meal, with fourteen people at the table. James had spent the morning out in the field with some of the men, and he sat on the men's side of the table, away from where Meg sat with the women. He didn't exactly blend in, she thought, with his expensive jeans and running shoes, now covered with mud, but he was enjoying himself.

The two of them had exchanged barely ten words since the day before. Apparently exhausted from whatever farmwork he had done, he had uncharacteristically gotten into bed at nine p.m. and fallen asleep almost instantly. The truth was, Meg had nothing to say to James at the moment, and he seemed to be taking advantage of the situation to stay away from her as well.

Several family members were taking a break after lunch, and Will, Eli, and Sam started a game of Monopoly. After helping clean up in the kitchen, Meg decided she would take Catherine's suggestion and lie down for a half hour to rest her back. Upstairs, she saw Lizzie, who had ducked out of the lunch cleanup, stretched out on her bed, arms crossed behind her head. She was staring at the ceiling.

Meg leaned against the doorjamb. "What's up?"

"Oh, if only there was something—anything —up," Lizzie answered, not bothering to look at her. "I'm so bored I want to scream."

"Where's your iPod?"

"Needs to be charged." Her voice grew more petulant. "But that would require an outlet, which would mean having electricity—which these freaks don't believe in."

Meg crossed her arms. "Hey, did you ever read *Tom Sawyer*? For school, maybe?"

Lizzie gave her mother a disdainful look. "Uh-uh."

"I saw it downstairs on the bookshelf. Definitely worth reading. It's a classic."

"Oh, a *classic*," Lizzie said with exaggerated awe. "Well, in that case . . ."

Meg ignored the crack. "That means it's good. Pick it up. I think you might enjoy it."

"This is what I've been reduced to: scrounging for old, boring books. Please just shoot me now. Really, I'm not kidding."

Meg turned around so Lizzie wouldn't see her smile. Her daughter was having to fend for herself without a cell phone, iPod, computer, or television. She might actually be driven to pick up a good book. Imagine. There were some unanticipated benefits to having a car accident, Meg thought as she shut her bedroom door behind her.

The day grew warm enough to melt whatever snow was left on the ground. By late afternoon, when the children had returned home from school, they congregated outside, where they were joined by a growing number of friends.

Watching from the porch, Meg observed Amish children arriving on foot, roller skates, or scooters. One teenage girl came on a large scooter with a basket in front and oversize wheels; she brought along a little girl and boy in a small low cart with wheels attached to the back.

All the children seemed to be bursting with energy, delighted to have this unusually warm, sunny day in the middle of winter. Most threw off their jackets or capes. The younger ones ran about, playing games, shouting and laughing. Meg spotted Rachel, the youngest Lutz child, talking and giggling with three other girls.

The teenagers, both boys and girls, assembled at the side of the house to play volleyball. It was quite a sight, Meg thought, all the girls in their richly colored dresses, their hair so neatly coiled into pinned-up braids. The boys, too, with their black pants and suspenders and similar haircuts.

She reflected that her children's friends also wore matching clothes, the same jeans, sneakers, and T-shirts. When she was a kid, she, too, had wanted to fit in by wearing the same clothes as the other kids. Not that her parents would pay for the stylish brands.

There had been rules then, even though unspoken, and there were rules now. It was different here, in that the clothing rules were dictated. They never changed. But at least everybody fit in, and no one had to struggle to do so.

In that way, it was a lot easier for an Amish teenager, at least when it came to getting dressed in the morning.

Sam was out there with Aaron and another boy who appeared to be around their age. The boy was on in line skates, making rapid circles around Sam and Aaron. Aaron held a long stick and kept tossing up small rocks, attempting to hit them as if they were baseballs. The boy spoke to Sam and pointed to a scooter leaning against the house. Sam raced over to grab it and was gone from sight.

"Mrs. Hobart?"

Meg turned around to see Amanda and Lizzie, zipping up her jacket, standing behind her.

"You said you want to go to the store. It is late, but we are going now. Do you want to go with us?"

"Oh, yes, thank you." Meg grabbed her coat. "Lizzie, you're coming?"

Her daughter shrugged. "It's something to do."

They followed Amanda to where Jonathan waited in what Meg now knew to be his buggy. He jumped out and extended a hand to help her up onto the front seat beside him. Amanda and Lizzie got in back.

They set out. Meg studied the young man next to her. Beneath his black hat, he had Catherine's blue eyes and brown hair. No doubt, Meg thought, he'd had the same light-blond hair as his younger siblings when he was a boy. Initially, she had found the bangs and bowl haircuts on the men incongruous, like children's hairstyles on grown-ups. She was getting used to them; they no longer seemed odd in the least.

"Do you do these deliveries every day?" Meg asked him.

"No, ma'am," he replied, his eyes on the road. "Depends on the season, how much we need to bring. A lot of things."

There was so much Meg wanted to ask him. She was dying to know how an eighteen-year-old Amish boy experienced the world.

"Please forgive me if I'm being rude, but I was wondering if you only work on your family farm or if you go to school, or anything like that."

He flicked the reins, and the horse picked up the pace. "We go to the school until eighth grade. Then we have a class one time every week. Like Eli. When we turn fifteen, we are done."

Meg realized her daughter was leaning forward in the back, trying to hear what Jonathan was saying.

"Sounds good to me," Lizzie interjected.

He turned his face a little to the side so she could hear him better. "It's necessary for us. We have to work. The American government gave permission so we can do it our way."

"All anybody talks about here is work. Don't you do anything for fun?"

"Lizzie," Meg admonished her, "that's so rude."

He smiled. "It's okay. Teenagers do a lot of things. After church, on Sunday nights, they have sings, and we have many ways to have a good time."

"What are 'sings'?" Lizzie asked.

"The girls and the boys go to someone's house, and they sing songs. It's a big social event. That's where many people find someone they like. Then they go out."

"Go out?" Lizzie echoed. "Like on dates?"

He smiled slightly. "Not like you would think, I guess. They spend time together."

"Do you mind if I ask whether you're dating someone?" Meg inquired.

"Oh my God, Mom!" yelled Lizzie as Jonathan turned beet red. "You did *not* just ask that!"

"I'm so sorry," Meg said. "That really was wrong of me. I'm very sorry."

For the first time, Amanda spoke up from the back. "It is okay, Mrs. Hobart. We never like to tell about those things to the grown-ups. When people are ready to be married, then they tell."

Lizzie faced Amanda. "So you never meet anybody besides the other kids who live here?"

Amanda hesitated. After a moment, Jonathan answered. "When we're sixteen, we can spend some time seeing the world if we want. We're allowed to visit new places and do different things. If we want to meet new people, we can.

That way we know when we are ready to join the church."

Meg was confused. "Wait—aren't you members of the church already?"

He looked at her with the same gaze as that of the younger children of the house: direct, guileless, and open. "No. That's one of the things about the Amish people. We believe you should be baptized when you decide to be a church member, as an adult. So you have time to go out and think it over. See what you're missing in the outside world."

"Did you do this, leave for a while?" Lizzie asked him. She turned to Amanda. "Wait— you're sixteen. Are you doing this?"

Jonathan answered again. "I tried some things, yes. But I knew what I wanted, and I was baptized."

Amanda's answer was firm. "I don't need to do anything different. I am happy as I am, and I will be baptized, too."

Lizzie spoke slowly. "I think I've heard about this someplace. There's a word for it, right?"

Amanda sighed. "The word you are thinking about is *rumspringa*. Many tourists ask about it. So, some kids maybe get their own apartment. They drive a car and wear the English clothes. We do things we are not allowed to do at home, and we see how we wish to live. Amish or not."

"Your parents are okay with this?" Meg asked.

Neither said anything. Finally, Jonathan answered. "Some kids decide fast, or they are like Amanda and they already know. Sometimes they take a long time to decide, and it causes a great deal of trouble. Like with our brother Benjamin. He's been gone now almost four months. My parents are very unhappy about him. They worry he'll be one of the ones who don't come back."

"Jonathan," Amanda reprimanded him, "you should not tell about this!"

That explained why they had the empty bedroom, Meg realized, the one that belonged to the son with all the sports equipment and posters. He was off somewhere, deciding about his future. Catherine had described him as being "away," with no further explanation.

So, Meg thought, even Amish parents sometimes had their guts taken out by their teenagers.

Jonathan looked annoyed at his sister's efforts to silence him but said nothing more. The horse trotted over the hilly roads, its hooves making their own music in the otherwise total quiet. The sun was setting, orange and pink streaking the sky. Meg guessed that by the time they got back to the farm, dinner would be ready, and everyone would gather for a silent prayer and the evening meal. She leaned back, relaxing into the jostling of the carriage, not thinking about anything at

169

all, and watched the sky transform into breath-taking purples and reds.

When they returned to the house, however, Meg had to acknowledge to herself that she had put off far too long making the call she had been dreading. Her parents were expecting her to arrive the day after tomorrow. That was out of the question. Still in her coat, she asked Catherine if she might use their telephone.

"It's in the shed around the back. Walk past the gazebo."

Meg thanked her and took a lantern outside. She pulled open the shed door and raised the lantern high enough to reveal a wealth of gardening tools and empty pots, all neatly arranged and well used but clean, ready be retrieved in the spring. Behind a wheelbarrow, she saw a small table with a telephone and answering machine, plus a white pad and several pencils. Meg almost laughed out loud, realizing she had somehow been expecting an antique phone, something tall and black, with an earpiece that she would hold up to her ear while shouting *"Operator, operator!"* This wasn't a cordless phone, and the answering machine looked fairly old, but they were both perfectly serviceable.

She stood the lantern on the table, where it cast an eerie glow on the shed's low ceiling, and dialed. Her mother picked up on the sixth ring. "Hello." As usual, the same flat tone.

"Hi, Mother, it's me," Meg said.

"What's wrong?"

Resisting the urge to scream at the assumption behind the question, Meg answered, "Nothing's wrong. I wanted to let you know we've had a little delay. We won't make it to you quite when I thought."

"Why?"

"It's not a big deal, really. The car needs some work, and we have to wait for it to be done."

"What do you mean 'needs some work'?" Her mother's suspicions were raised. "You had an accident, didn't you?"

Congratulations, Meg wanted to say. You got it in one. "Just a small mishap" was what she said instead. "The car ran off the road. Everyone's fine, and it'll be fixed. But they have to order a part or something, and it could take a few days. Maybe even a week."

"A week? That's not some small mishap."

Meg closed her eyes and rested her head in one hand.

"Will insurance pay for it?" her mother wanted to know.

Nothing about the well-being of her grandchildren, Meg noticed. "Yes, the money's not a problem."

Her mother let out a short snort of derision. "It's hardly surprising. That old car wasn't in any shape to make this trip. You knew that."

"We didn't have much choice, if you recall," Meg retorted, knowing she was perilously close to inviting an argument.

Her mother chose to ignore the invitation. "Where are you?"

"We're in Pennsylvania."

"What on earth are you doing there?"

"This is where it happened. I can give you the phone number where we're staying in case you need to reach us."

"You're in a hotel? How can you afford that?"

Oh, boy, here it comes, thought Meg. This is going to be a moment to remember. "No. We're staying with an Amish family. They're lovely people. And they refuse to let us pay them for anything."

There was dead silence on the phone.

"Mother? Did you hear me?"

"I heard you, but I don't believe you."

Meg only sighed.

"*Amish* people?" her mother asked. "You mean the ones without electricity and the weird clothes? The ones who refuse to live in the real world? I didn't even think those people still exist."

"They do. And they're very nice."

"Well, Margaret, that's a new one on me." Her mother made no attempt to minimize her monumental disapproval. "What are you doing, mixing with people like that? And you have the *children* with you? You let them be exposed to this cult?"

Meg bristled. "You have no right to say that. They are most certainly not a cult. You don't know anything about them!"

"I know that people don't let strangers stay in their house for free, I can tell you that! They want something from you. Are they talking religious things to you? Don't you let them try to convert you."

Meg thought that if she had the proper medical instruments, she would be able to see her blood pressure skyrocketing. "Stop it, Mother, stop it right now!" She had promised herself she wouldn't yell, but she couldn't help it. "You have no right to talk like that. These people are just nice, period. Can't you imagine such a thing, people being nice?"

A deafening silence.

"If they're so nice," her mother said, "perhaps they'd like to take you in permanently."

Checkmate. If Meg didn't capitulate, and fast, she would have no place to go once the car got fixed. Deep breaths, she told herself, deep breaths.

She didn't bother taking any deep breaths but rushed out the words before any further damage could be done. "Okay, Mother, why don't we just figure the car will be fixed in a couple of days, and we'll be on our way to you. I'll make sure the children aren't exposed to anything radical or dangerous." She lightened her tone, certain the strain of doing so would take five years off her life. "We're looking forward to getting back to the original plan. We'll be there in time to celebrate Christmas together."

That seemed to throw off her mother, who apparently hadn't given any thought to the approach of the holiday. "Your father and I stopped buying Christmas trees a long time ago. And I know you can't afford to waste whatever money you have left on a bunch of useless presents. So I'm not sure what celebrating you're planning on."

"Maybe I'll make a cake . . ." Meg trailed off, unable to keep up this conversation for another minute. "Well, we'll all be together. So I'll call you when I know more."

"Yes, I think you had better."

"Thanks, Mother."

"Margaret, you be careful of these people. You understand?"

"I understand."

"Fine. Goodbye."

Grabbing the lantern, Meg opened the door and stepped outside. I'll count until ten, she said to herself, and if my head doesn't explode by then, I'll know I'm okay.

Chapter 10

Lizzie grimaced at the tall laminated menu. "Why aren't all these people dead of heart attacks? I can't even believe what they eat."

James smiled. "Not exactly like the restaurants back home, is it? No arugula salad, say, or grilled fish."

Lizzie wrinkled her nose in distaste. "Ick. It's not like I eat that stuff, either."

"They really love their ham here, you gotta give them that," Will added as he scanned the offerings.

The restaurant was a sea of empty tables. It was lunchtime on a Wednesday afternoon in December, so Meg was hardly surprised that the cavernous restaurant was practically deserted. Other than a young couple with twin toddlers and an elderly couple lingering over coffee, she didn't see any other customers. This place must serve a billion tourists in the summer, she thought. Which was probably a good thing.

Delivering the pies the day before, she had come to understand what a strange relationship the Amish had with tourists. Or at least it seemed strange to her. While the tourists invaded the peaceful existence, they also brought in money to sustain it. During the ride, Jonathan had explained that the increasing price of land made it difficult for the younger generations to buy property near their families. As much as the Amish valued farming, they'd turned to other professions to support themselves, and many had taken jobs outside their community. Selling food, crafts, furniture, and the like to tourists had become an important source of income.

Meg didn't know how all the Amish felt about it, but some had obviously made their peace with it. If tourism brought in critical dollars, then Meg supposed they had to work with it, not against it.

The Lutzes' solution combined farming with making food and other things to sell. They didn't sell directly to the public but to shops and bakeries. The store where they dropped off the apple pies clearly catered to tourists. When they'd arrived, the owner was locking the front door, closing for the night. Jonathan, Amanda, and Lizzie brought the pies in through a back door while Meg roamed the store aisles, perusing an array of crafts. Amid a seeming ocean of goods, she paused to examine colorful place mats and napkins, candles, dried-flower arrangements, the summer straw hats worn by Amish men, and small, soft faceless dolls in Amish dress. She grew hungry just reading the labels on the endless packages of homemade food, everything from apple butter and pickles to candy and chutneys.

By the time they got back to the Lutz farm, everyone was assembling in the kitchen for supper. Meg let herself be carried away on the gentle wave of quiet goodwill at the supper table and the sight of all the activity in the room afterward. While she cleaned up with the other women, the young cousins from next door and several children she hadn't seen joined the Lutz children for the evening. Lizzie and Will even sat in on some board games, while Sam made Christmas cards with Aaron and Rachel near a crackling fire. Curious, Meg observed them using glitter, rubber stamps, and markers to make their own cards, none of which featured Santa or presents but, rather, simple religious words or themes. Yes, Barbara confirmed when Meg asked her as they wiped down the kitchen counters, they did send Christmas cards to their faraway relatives and some English friends. Sam, Meg noted with a touch of sadness, made several cards but didn't personalize them or take any to send; apparently, he wasn't interested in keeping up with the kids back in Charlotte.

It had been a peaceful, happy evening, ending with pretzels and ice cream for everyone. Meg was still full from the night before when she came down in the morning to find a table laden with oatmeal, cold cereal, eggs, bacon, hash browns, muffins, warm bread, and butter.

After breakfast, James and she agreed that they had to give the Lutzes a break from including the five of them in the household meals, even if it meant dipping into their meager funds. Not to mention that her children were still complaining about how few things they could stand to eat at the meals. When Meg informed Catherine that they would be going out for lunch, Catherine protested but eventually gave in. She suggested that Jonathan drop them off at the restaurant and retrieve them later. Meg was glad they had come, even if it looked as though this wasn't going to be quite the success she'd hoped in terms of her family finding something to eat.

"I have to tell you," James said, peering over his menu, "I've been doing some work with the men—not even anything big, mind you—and I've been starved when we get in for dinner. These people don't need gyms or treadmills, and they don't need diets." He grimaced. "Although the cholesterol is going to kill me."

"Their cooking comes from another time and place, before anybody cared about that stuff," Meg remarked.

Sam, seated at Meg's left, hadn't said anything since they sat down. "They come from Germany," he offered. "In the beginning, I mean."

They all looked at him in surprise.

"How would *you* know?" Will asked.

He shrugged. "I talk to Aaron and Eli. Don't you talk to anybody?"

"I guess I'm not as popular as you, big shot" was Will's snide reply.

Sam went on, "People call them Pennsylvania Dutch, but they don't even speak Dutch. They talk in a German dialogue."

" 'Dialogue'?" asked James. "You mean 'dialect'?"

Sam nodded. "Yeah, I guess so. In church, they talk in real German. Plus, they learn English. So that's, like, three languages. Pretty cool."

"Definitely," said Meg, impressed with her son's fact-finding.

"A long time ago, back in Germany, people wanted to kill them. That's how they wound up here."

Lizzie muttered under her breath, "Probably wanted to kill them 'cause their clothes are so ugly."

Will let out a guffaw.

James's eyes flared with anger. "You kids are the most obnoxious, ungrateful—What is *with* you?"

"Oh, come on, Dad," Will said. "Seriously, you think you would have liked being here when you were our age?"

"Okay, that's a fair question." James was quiet

for a few seconds, considering. "I might not have liked it," he said finally, "but I know I would have kept my opinions to myself. I would never make fun of people right under their noses, or act like it was all too much to be born, the way you and Lizzie are acting."

"I think these people are great," Sam said. "They're so nice."

"What do you know?" Lizzie snapped. "You're just running around with a puppy and your new fake grandpa, so you think the world is suddenly a beautiful place."

Meg stared at her. "When did you get so cynical?"

The waitress appeared at James's elbow. She was a teenager, with enormous hoop earrings and dark hair pulled back into a tight, high ponytail. "Hey, there, you folks ready?" she asked.

James looked apologetic. "Can you give us another minute?"

"Sure thing. Just sing out if you have any questions." She left, her ponytail bouncing behind her.

Lizzie mimicked her in disgust. " *'Just sing out if you have any questions.'* Is anybody in this place for real? I feel like we're among the pod people or something."

"They're not pod people!" Sam's voice rose with emotion. "Aaron and Eli are, like, the best guys I ever met. And they're so lucky to be in that family."

There was a moment of quiet, then, without another word, Lizzie burst into tears. Everyone sat, stunned, as she buried her face in her hands, sobbing. Meg jumped up and came around the table, kneeling to wrap her arms around her daughter. "Lizzie, what on earth is it? What's going on?"

Lizzie raised her face, flushed and wet. "Yeah, they're lucky because they're actually *in* a family. We used to be a family, too." She looked briefly at Meg, her voice cracking with the effort of holding back tears. "You and Dad used to love each other. Now you hate each other. We're nothing but a bunch of homeless people, and nobody loves anybody anymore. We're just sponging off of these people until we can go to our horrible new lives with more people who don't love us and who we don't love." She covered her face again as she sobbed.

"Dear God," James breathed.

Meg felt her throat close up, as if she couldn't take a breath. She wrapped her arms more closely around Lizzie, feeling her shake with the force of her sobs.

I can't believe I could be so stupid, Meg berated herself. How could I have thought the kids would just get in line and do whatever we said. No problems, no worries, as long as we patted them on the head and told them how we expected them to behave. As if, by following a few simple rules, they could overlook the fact that their world had exploded.

She met James's pained eyes across the table. It wasn't the house that was the problem, nor the money, nor the moving. That stuff the kids could deal with—not easily, maybe, but eventually. It was the fact that they could plainly see the rift between their parents. That was the worst thing of all. She knew that she and James had done a terrible job of pretending to get along, but the children understood that their parents' marriage was hanging by a thread.

She turned to Will, who looked miserable as he continued making believe he was absorbed in running his finger around the rim of his water glass. Sam was watching her, clutching his napkin in both hands, his eyes brimming with tears.

What could she tell them? That she and James weren't splitting up? She couldn't make that promise. That everything would be great when they got to her parents'? Not likely, and they wouldn't believe her anyway.

She rubbed Lizzie's back. "Don't worry, sweetie. It'll all work out," she murmured.

"Will it?" James asked.

She gave him a murderous look. He stared right back at her.

No one spoke. No one moved.

This, she realized, this very moment, was the lowest point of her marriage, her family, and, quite possibly, her life.

Chapter 11

Sam paused on the front porch to give his mother a hug. She stopped sweeping, bending to kiss him on the cheek. "Have fun, pumpkin," she told him. "And put on your gloves."

He ignored her advice, running after Aaron and Rachel to get into Old Samuel's buggy. Today Sam was going to be a guest at the school. He'd been thrilled to be treated like the other two children that morning. Catherine had handed him a silver lunch box and a glass bottle full of soup. Then she sent him off with a pat on the head. Once Sam was safely ensconced in the rig, Old Samuel nodded at a waving Meg, then snapped the reins. The horse set out at a slow trot.

Meg resumed sweeping the front steps. As the week had passed, she had been assuming additional chores around the house. Typically, Barbara Lutz cleaned up the porch and front yard, making sure the grounds remained neat. When Meg's soreness from the accident had almost completely dissipated, she insisted on taking over that job. She hadn't expected to enjoy the early-morning quiet as much as she did, punctuated only by a dog's bark or a brief commotion in the chicken house. The broom's rhythmic noise against the porch was soothing. She pictured the ornate front door at their house back in Charlotte, knowing full well she never would have enjoyed sweeping those steps. Was it only in this environment that such satisfaction could be found? she wondered. Was there any way to hold on to the simple pleasure of a job well done? Maybe a person needed to have more simple jobs to do, until they crowded out the ridiculous things that typically took up so much time.

Moving toward the side of the house, she saw Racer stretched out on his side on a brown patch of ground. "Hey, boy," she called.

He stayed exactly as he was, but she was absurdly gratified by the two thumps of his tail she received in reply.

She finished up and put the broom away inside before heading over to Annie's house. Today the women planned to bake two hundred muffins, an assortment of blueberry, cranberry, and corn. Meg would do whatever they assigned her. Being around the daily baking was making her itch to do some of her own, but so far she had refrained from asking. She did not want to interfere with their schedules or, worse yet, cause any additional work.

As she walked, she wondered what kind of

morning James was experiencing. Things between them had become even more tense since their lunch in the restaurant, and all five of them seemed unable to deal with it. Each of them acted as if it had never happened. She and her husband were at a complete impasse. She wondered what on earth it would take to change things.

James had gone off early this morning with David, Jonathan, and Eli to help butcher meat in a neighbor's barn. Meg admired the perfect logic of the activities here. Anything having to do with planting and harvesting took top priority; whatever else had to get done was scheduled around those months. That explained everything, down to why most of their weddings were held in November and December, when obligations in the field were at a minimum.

Meg didn't care to know too many specific details about the butchering, but she had been surprised by how enthusiastic James was about pitching in. Amazing that the man who once fussed over wine in a restaurant was now hefting a pitchfork, wielding a cleaver, and slogging around in manure wearing borrowed boots. She wasn't sure if he had embraced all this farm labor or if he was using it as a distraction from their troubles. At the very least, she thought, it was a welcome delay in reaching his in-laws' house, and she couldn't blame him for feeling that way. He seemed to have become awfully comfortable, though, with their being the house-guests who wouldn't leave.

Of course, she didn't know what James was thinking because they were barely talking. All this division of labor between the sexes, all the hours spent apart, made an argument with your spouse unlikely, she thought. But once you'd gotten into one, it was also a good way to avoid dealing with it any further.

Entering Annie's house, Meg spotted Lizzie and Barbara in a corner of the living room. Without electricity, all the Hobart children had been going to sleep a lot earlier than they were used to. As a result, they were wide awake in the mornings. Even Lizzie, queen of the late sleepers, had adjusted her internal clock.

Barbara held a hand-painted plate, removed from a display of dishes in an enormous oak breakfront, and was pointing out the fine details of its pattern to Lizzie. Meg went over to them. "Good morning, Barbara, Lizzie."

Lizzie glanced up at her mother without much interest, but Barbara flashed her usual big smile. "Good morning, Meg. I'm showing Lizzie what I hope to get after the wedding. As gifts. I have some dishes such as these that I have gotten over the years, but I hope to get the rest."

"Mostly, they get stuff for the kitchen and the house," Lizzie added. "They don't ask for any fun things. Fancy dishes are, like, the biggest deal when it comes to something special."

Barbara laughed. "Lizzie is having trouble with this idea. She says a bride could ask for anything, but we are happy to get mops and pitchers."

Lizzie shrugged. "I mean, I never heard of getting a shovel as a wedding gift."

"The English maybe like different things, that's all," Barbara said.

"You know," Meg said to her daughter, "we have wedding showers, and that's often all about things for the house. And people get lots of appliances for wedding gifts. You're just thinking of all the extra, unnecessary things." She laughed. "Like the million vases and candlesticks people gave Dad and me when we got married. How often do I use those?" She corrected herself. "How often *did* I use those? Or all those crystal glasses, which were almost too fragile to handle."

"I don't mean to sound greedy or anything," Lizzie said. "It's just that this is the one time you can flat out ask for cool things and nobody minds."

Barbara put an arm around Lizzie. "When you get married, you will decide what is important to you. But this is how we do it here. It makes sense for us."

"I should join the others now," Meg said. "Want to come, Lizzie?"

"Nope."

Meg turned to leave. "See you later."

Midmorning, everybody congregated back in Catherine's house. The families sat down for lunch, their usual silent prayer followed by yet another enormous meal starting with meat loaf, lima beans with molasses and ketchup, and the ever-present bread and butter. After lunch, work began in earnest to transform the barn across the street at Joseph's house for the wedding. The enormous space was better suited to a large event than David and Catherine's barn, but the Lutz men, James, and a crowd of men from the community got to work framing an extension to make space for all the tables and benches that would arrive on Monday. Will and Lizzie disappeared, but Meg and the women went back to Annie's home to sort a steady stream of arriving dishes, glasses, silverware, and pots and pans, all lent and delivered by neighbors and friends.

"You know," Catherine said to Meg as they sorted platters by size, "we would like to ask you and James to be among the people who cook and serve at the wedding."

Meg smiled at her. "You know you can count on us."

Catherine picked up several pitchers, cradling them in her arms, and moved to put them in a different spot. Joseph's wife, Sue, had come into the kitchen with a box of coffee cups and was unpacking them near Meg. She moved closer to speak to her.

"We love to celebrate happy times like a wedding," she explained to Meg. "Everybody wants to be part of it, to help make the food, but only about thirty people can. It is good for you to have this big honor, to be asked to cook?"

Meg turned to her. She'd had no idea. "Yes, of course," she said. "We're very honored."

Sue's smile was gentle as she moved away. Thank you, Meg thought. Without that little tip-off, she never would have appreciated the significance of Catherine's request. She made a mental note to tell James.

When Catherine returned, Meg smiled at her with genuine warmth. "You have been so good to us," she said. "I can never repay you."

Catherine frowned. "Repay me? What a bad idea. That makes it sound like business."

Barbara walked by them, carrying a bucket and some clean rags.

"She starts washing today." Catherine's eyes followed her daughter. "Our house, Joseph's house. Wherever the guests will come." She sighed.

"What is it?" asked Meg.

"No, nothing. I am just—you know, a mother can't help it. It is a little sad that she is moving to her husband's family farm."

"Oh, yes," Meg said sympathetically.

"It is the right thing, and I want her to do it. It is not so far away, just about ten miles, so I am very grateful. But it is a big change, your daughter leaving your house for always."

Meg nodded, trying to imagine how she would feel when her children left to be on their own. She could guess that, as much as she wanted to see them grow up to be independent, it would be devastating.

"If only my son Benjamin would decide. I don't even know if he will come home for the wedding or . . ." Catherine stopped.

It took Meg a moment to recall that Benjamin was the son who was out in the world, finding out if he wanted to remain a member of the Amish community. How painful this must be for Catherine and her husband. Meg lightly put a comforting hand on her shoulder, and Catherine put her own hand over it.

"Surely he'll want to—" Meg was interrupted by Leah, who appeared behind her. Where had she been standing?

"Catherine, please to come with me." Leah's accent was heavy and her words generally difficult for Meg to understand. She understood these, though, and the disapproval behind them.

Meg tried to pretend she wasn't watching as the two women retreated to the farthest point in the room. She didn't have to hear them to interpret Leah's stern expression and rapid speaking—no doubt in their own language—as criticism of Catherine. When Leah, seemingly unconsciously, briefly pointed in Meg's direction, Meg knew she was the cause of this tongue-lashing.

Abashed, Meg kept her face down as Catherine returned, slightly pink in the cheeks but otherwise composed.

"I'm so sorry," Meg whispered. "I got you in trouble with your mother-in-law, didn't I?"

Catherine came very close to her, reaching her arm across Meg to pick up a large bowl. She turned her head so no one could see her answering. "We don't speak of our problems to outsiders," she whispered back. "For a minute I forgot to think of you as an outsider. As my little Rachel would say, silly me."

Meg paused in what she was doing, so surprised she forgot to pretend they weren't having a conversation. Catherine grabbed some more bowls and hastened away as someone called her name. Before Meg could think about how wonderful Catherine's words had made her feel, she was distracted by Lizzie's appearance at the door, Amanda trailing behind her.

Meg's eyes met her daughter's, and she raised a questioning eyebrow. Lizzie shrugged as she approached.

"I'm here to help," Lizzie said. "Amanda said we had to. She said we'd all be in trouble if we didn't."

Meg sighed. "You wouldn't have thought of helping on your own?"

"*Mo-om!* I'm here, aren't I? What do I have to do?"

"Well, Barbara has a bucket. I think she's washing furniture. You like her, so maybe you want to help with that."

Lizzie made a face. "I don't like anybody *that* much."

Meg was growing impatient. "Why don't you go over there and ask Sue what needs to be done."

Lizzie was assigned to count the forks, knives, and spoons, separating them into piles. Meg was pleased to see someone had put Will to work as well. He came through the door struggling under the weight of split logs. She watched him unload the wood near the fireplace. Something was stirring in her memory, although she wasn't sure what.

It came to her. This past Thanksgiving in Charlotte. It was only last month, but it felt like another life. She had set the table, and the children had helped bring in chairs. She remembered the hours she'd spent orchestrating the placement of her sterling silver salt and pepper dishes. As if it mattered in the least, she couldn't help thinking now.

Someone set another box of serving platters beside her, and she began to unpack them. That had been their last holiday, she recalled, the last huge feast they had shared as a family. It was the day she had found out what James had done with the family's money. It was the last day of their old lives.

"Watch it, stupid!"

At the sound of Will's voice, Meg turned around to see what was going on. Lizzie, carrying a large basket piled high with serving utensils, had apparently tripped over Will's foot as he knelt to stack wood near the fireplace. Her daughter had recovered her balance just in time to avoid falling.

"*I* should watch it? You're the one whose foot is sticking out," Lizzie snapped. Her tone was disgusted. "Jerk."

All the faces in the room turned toward the two teenagers. Mortified, Meg practically ran across the room.

Will had risen to confront his sister more directly. "We can't all be worrying about staying out of Your Majesty's way."

Meg reached them and took each one by an arm firmly enough to communicate that she meant business. "Why don't we discuss this outside?" she said as calmly as she could manage. She hustled them the mercifully few feet to the front door. The instant they were outside, each one started yelling to Meg about the other.

"Both of you be quiet this instant!" she hissed.

194

They stopped talking.

"Do you see the kids here treating one another like you two do?" she demanded. "No. They are nice. They are kind. They are even, believe it or not, respectful."

Two sets of shoulders sagged as they realized they were going to get a long lecture.

"I'm so sick of your behavior, I don't even know how to describe the way I feel," Meg said. "You embarrass me. Worse, you embarrass yourselves." She surprised them by turning away. "I wonder if you can even understand that."

She opened the door and went inside without looking back. Had she been alone, she realized, she probably would have given in to the self-recriminations that were flooding her mind. She wanted to weep with disappointment over her children's ongoing bad behavior and for what-ever hand she may have had in it. But the women here didn't seem to know the meaning of self-pity, and she knew not one of them would stop working to feel sorry for herself. They put one foot in front of the other no matter what.

She might not be Amish, but she could learn a lesson from them. She smoothed her hair and composed her face. She didn't try to adopt a cheerful smile but quietly returned to her task. From the other women's behavior, it was impossible to tell that anyone had noticed her children's bickering. Meg was immediately absorbed back into the conversation.

The sun was beginning to set when she went outside to take a break, a steaming mug of coffee in hand. The kitchen had been growing progressively hotter, but the extreme cold instantly made her appreciate the coffee's warmth. Not having put on her coat, she held one arm tightly across her midsection, shivering a bit while she sipped on the hot drink.

Out on the main road, she spotted Will and Eli, both on skateboards. Will, she noticed, was using his own, the one she had salvaged. She was glad she had. A number of the children here had skateboards, so it had been useful for Will to have his. At the moment he and Eli were clearly racing, both speeding from some unknown starting point. Meg stifled her natural impulse to yell out at Will to slow down, knowing he would never do it, especially considering he was in the middle of an actual race. She just held the mug's handle a bit more tightly. They were really flying, she thought. When they passed the designated finish line, they both slowed down and then stopped sharply. Eli held up his fist in a momentary gesture of victory.

Meg watched Will skate over to talk animatedly to Eli, who nodded. She could guess that her son wasn't willing to concede defeat so easily; he would be making sure he got another crack at winning. Reversing direction, the boys aligned themselves side by side, and she could hear Will's voice as he shouted "Go!"

This time Meg could almost feel her son's determination as he increased his speed, his head slightly lowered, his body locked into position. Eli was going fast, too, but his body didn't communicate the same frantic desire to win. Sure enough, Will sailed over the finish line well ahead of Eli. Will jumped off his skateboard, repeatedly pumping his fists in the air. Eli came to a full stop, one foot on the ground. He appeared to be patiently waiting for Will to finish his strutting. Then, with a wave of his arm, Will challenged Eli to two out of three. They took off down the street once more.

Eli got there first, just barely. He simply bent over, picked up his skateboard, and stood there. Will brought his skateboard to a screeching halt, jumped off, and gave it a good kick. Meg watched her son, his arm's jerky gesticulations indicating his displeasure as he undoubtedly ranted about whatever he believed had caused him to lose. Eli shrugged. Will went on for a bit more until the other boy nodded toward his parents' house and started walking. Will stared after him. Eli stopped, turned back, and put out a hand as if to ask whether Will was coming. Meg observed Will take a moment, then grab his skateboard and drag himself after the other boy.

As soon as he caught up, Eli leaned in to him and said something that made Will laugh.

Meg sighed. All boys may like to win, she reflected, but not all boys need to rub their opponents' faces in it when they do. Will had been treated to an example of a gracious winner. She hoped with all her heart that he had taken note.

The screen door opened, and Catherine stuck her head out. "We are done here," she said to Meg. "It is time to go back to my house now."

Meg nodded and stopped inside to wash her coffee mug. It was almost dark and growing still colder as the two of them walked toward the house. Talking along the way, Meg learned Barbara's soon-to-be-in-laws ran a dairy farm, but Moses, the man Barbara was marrying, was their youngest son, and they were elderly, ready to retire. They were handing over the main responsibilities for the farm to Moses and Barbara, who would move into the main house. His parents had built an attached house for themselves, which Meg learned was called a *Grossdaadi Haus*, just like the one in which Leah and Old Samuel lived.

"This is how it happened with David and me," Catherine finished as they came into her house and hung up their outer clothes on the wall pegs. "His parents lived in this part before we were married. We built the house across the road for our son Joseph when he married Sue, and that is the biggest one of all of them."

Meg tried to imagine having in-laws living in an attachment to her house in Charlotte. Thinking of Leah, she gazed at Catherine with new admiration.

Almost as if she had read Meg's mind, Catherine said, "We respect the elders of the community very much. It is a good thing when you grow old here—no one is alone, we are all together."

Ashamed of her uncharitable thoughts, Meg nodded.

"Mommy!" Sam came bounding into the room. "I thought you would never get home! I want to tell you about my day at school."

"I can't wait to hear." Meg hugged him tightly. "Let's sit down, and you'll tell me everything."

"It was great!" he announced as they settled themselves on the couch.

"Doesn't Daddy want to hear this? We should get him," Meg said.

"I already told him in the barn. I'm sorry, but I couldn't wait anymore, and you just weren't anywhere."

She smiled. "Okay, go ahead."

"It was soooo different from at home," Sam gushed. "The teacher's name is Sarah, and they call her that, her first name. There was a fire in this old-fashioned stove to warm up the room, and she put some of the lunch stuff on it so it would be hot later. Like my soup."

"Clever," Meg said.

"Yeah, one kid had a baked potato wrapped in foil stuff, and it cooked right there by lunch!"

Meg nodded. "I like that idea. Neat trick."

"Sarah was super nice. So, all these kids are together, all different ages, up to the eighth grade." Sam's voice dropped to an awed whisper. "They're really well behaved, you wouldn't believe it. I mean, it was crazy. I know Mrs. Whitford wouldn't believe it."

Meg smiled. Mrs. Whitford had been Sam's teacher in Charlotte.

"They said prayers and sang songs. Some of them were in German. I didn't know any of them, so I just sat there next to Aaron, trying to look like I knew what was going on. As if!"

"I'm sure they didn't expect you to," Meg pointed out.

"They were so nice to me." The words came rushing out. "Everybody did different things, 'cause of what age they were. Big kids helped littler kids. They did math and reading, all stuff like I do. We had recess and played games. I got to play darts. It was awesome." Sam stood up. "I could see it—going to school just till eighth grade, working on the farm." He looked thoughtful, then shrugged. "But I'm not Amish, and we don't have a farm, so there you go," he finished.

"I gotta find Old Samuel. Y'know, he actually *whittles*. I've never seen anybody whittle in real life. He's going to show me how. And I have to find Rufus."

"See you later, then."

"It was a super-cool day, Mom. Bye." He ran off.

A super-cool day indeed, she thought.

Dinner was delayed that evening as they waited for Jonathan and James to get back. They had gone to check on the progress of the Mustang after David told them a message from the repair shop had been left on the answering machine for James. When they finally arrived and everyone sat down for the meal, James announced that he had been summoned to the repair shop only to okay the paint job. The car wouldn't be ready for another week.

Meg watched the reactions on her children's faces. Predictably, Sam looked delighted, while Will and Lizzie were horrified. Meg herself had mixed feelings. They should be getting back to their own lives, yet she knew how wrenching it would be to leave the Lutz family. She had to admit she did not feel as bad about the delay as perhaps she should.

Later on, when she and James found themselves alone in their bedroom, she questioned him further about the car.

"The guy wanted to make sure I was okay

about his just repainting the damaged part of the car instead of painting the whole thing," he said. "It looked great, but we're still stuck. What would happen if we weren't here with these people?"

"They've been amazing," Meg said. "Feeding us, lending us everything we need."

"I know, I know," James retorted. "You don't have to remind me that we have no money. That we're charity cases because of me."

"That's not what I meant," Meg said, stiffening. "Not everything is an indictment of you."

"Well, that's how it feels."

"Maybe that's because it should be," she snapped. "You have yet to say or do anything to show that you even get it. That you have a clue about what you did."

"I know what I did."

"I mean what you did *to us*. Me and the kids. You don't seem to get that at all."

"What do you want me to do, Meg? I'm sorry, but I can't replace the money."

She glared at him. "It's not about the money, I keep trying to tell you that. It's that I can't trust you. On any level. So where does that leave us?"

His reply was angry and abrupt. "Damned if I know." He left the room, and she listened to his footsteps go down the stairs.

Meg didn't want to sit alone in the bedroom, thinking about how angry she was. She decided to go downstairs and see if anyone might be around. What she found were six children she didn't recognize playing with the younger Lutz children and her son Sam, all of them illuminated by the fire and the glow of kerosene lamps. They were spread out around the room snacking on bowls of popcorn.

Meg saw four Amish women she hadn't encountered seated at the kitchen table with Catherine, Leah, and Amanda, most of them working on a quilt.

"Oh, excuse me," Meg said, pausing in the doorway. "I didn't mean to interrupt."

Catherine gestured to a chair. "Come in, Meg."

Meg sat at a little distance from the group so she wouldn't be in their way. Introductions were made. It appeared they were fairly far along with the quilt, which had numerous pieces of fabric sewn into intricate patterns on a black background. She craned her neck to study it. "That is absolutely beautiful," she exclaimed.

One of the women, who appeared to be in her seventies, looked up to peer at Meg. Her English was heavily accented, but Meg could make it out. "It is for the schoolteacher. A Christmas present from the families."

"Sarah," Meg recalled aloud.

The woman smiled. "Yes. You know of her?"

"My son spent today at the school. He enjoyed it very much."

One of the other women looked up at her. "My daughter told me about the little English boy with Aaron."

Meg nodded. "Yes, Sam is my son."

The second woman said something to the others in their own language. They all smiled as they continued to work.

Catherine turned to Meg. "She is explaining how my father-in-law calls him Young Samuel." She was sewing the hem of a white apron.

"No quilting for you?" Meg asked.

"Not tonight," Catherine answered. "This is for Barbara to wear at her wedding. After this, I will finish work on her cape. She wears special white clothes. They look like our other clothes, but new ones, for this use only."

"Almost only . . ." Leah put in, without taking her eyes off her work.

"True." Catherine nodded. "After the wedding they are put away, and she will be buried in them."

Meg hoped her face didn't betray her surprise at this piece of information. She turned the idea over in her mind. She supposed it all fit, the tight linking of family traditions.

"Do you also make these quilts to sell, or only for yourselves?" Meg asked.

"Both." The older woman answered again for all of them. "We maybe do some different patterns for the tourists, things they like. They are often on white backgrounds."

Catherine went on, "We sew many different designs. Like Wedding Ring, which is circles that are locking together. We have many kinds."

Another woman glanced up at Meg. "Can you sew?"

"No, not really." Meg tried not to feel abashed by her ignorance of what was a most basic skill to these people. "I can knit a little," she added with a laugh, "but just enough to make a scarf, I'm afraid."

Leah, who was sitting next to Amanda, leaned over to her and whispered something into her granddaughter's ear. Amanda nodded, excused herself, and left the room. She returned a few minutes later with a skein of dark-blue wool and two knitting needles.

"Maybe you would like to make scarves for your children," Leah said. "I see they do not have."

Meg didn't know what made her feel more taken aback—the fact that Leah would do such a kind thing for her, or that she had bothered to notice Meg's children weren't dressed properly and cared enough to do something to rectify the situation.

"Thank you very, very much," Meg said to her. "It's a lot warmer in our home state, and the children don't have the proper clothes here. This means a great deal to me."

Leah gave a little nod. "I have more of this blue wool" was all she said.

Now, thought Meg, let's hope I can remember how to do it.

Happily, her fingers seemed to begin casting on by themselves, and she became engrossed in knitting. The women worked mainly in silence, but occasionally they shared an observation. When the subject turned to Barbara's wedding on Tuesday, they became more animated, discussing what had yet to be done.

"Soon it will be finished, a wonderful memory," one of the women said to Catherine. "You will go back to visiting."

Meg looked at her inquiringly.

"In the cold months," Catherine explained, "we do much visiting with family and our friends. The wedding keeps us busy now, but after, we will go to people's houses, and they will come to ours."

"Especially Barbara and Moses," Amanda added. "They go on so many visits after. That is when many people give them the wedding presents, and it's time to see a lot of the people who came."

Everyone resumed their tasks in silence. In the background, the children moved about, most of them in their socks, their conversation punctuated by loud bursts of laughter. Every so often a young child would approach the table and look at Meg before whispering a question. Sam, she saw, was fully absorbed in a game of

Sorry with two boys she didn't recognize.

"Do you do a lot of visiting with relatives?" the woman who had just spoken asked Meg.

She shook her head. "We don't have many. My parents are the only ones, really." She hesitated. "Unfortunately, we don't get along well with them."

Catherine raised her face, concern in her eyes. "This is true?"

"No, no, I shouldn't have said that," Meg answered. Why had she felt the need to air her personal problems?

Sensing her reluctance to discuss it further, the women changed the subject. The evening slipped by in what seemed like minutes. Meg had made substantial progress on her scarf when it dawned on her that she should really give these women time to themselves. I've been enjoying myself far too much, she thought, wrapping up her knitting. The women must have things they want to discuss that they can't, or won't, talk about in front of me.

"It has been lovely to meet all of you," Meg said. "Please excuse me now. I must go to bed."

They nodded, but no one stopped what they were doing.

"Sam," she called out to her son, "finish up and come upstairs."

"Okay, okay," he called back. "In a minute."

Meg headed to the staircase, holding her knitting. As she climbed the steps, she wondered if she was intentionally getting too involved in these people's lives. She was allowing herself to be lulled into ignoring her situation, had even complained about her problems.

This was not her world, and it never would be. Sooner or later she would have to face the mess that was her real life.

Chapter 12

On Saturday morning Meg looked out her bedroom window to see the countryside completely covered with a soft, thick quilt of snow. Everything—houses, barns, trees—stood partially hidden beneath at least half a foot of snow, all sounds muffled by its weight. Tree branches sagged beneath the heavy snowfall. The temperature must have dropped further in the hours before dawn, and many of the trees were decorated by glistening ice that sparkled when the pale sunlight managed to break through the clouds. The magnificent serenity nearly took her breath away.

She tore herself from the view to wash her face and brush her hair. Getting dressed in the mornings was considerably faster here than it had been at home, primarily because the Amish didn't keep mirrors in the house. The only time Meg looked at herself was when she picked up the tiny makeup mirror she had in her own purse. There was no way of fussing over how her clothing looked. After a day or two, she had abandoned the idea of putting on makeup altogether, not only because she couldn't see well enough in her mirror to do it properly, but because it made her uncomfortable around all the other women with their fresh-scrubbed faces. By this point, the notion of wearing a face full of makeup struck her as faintly ridiculous, as if she were slathering dirt on herself.

She didn't know how to do the hairstyle favored by the women here—what she thought of as a version of French braids tied back—but she had taken to gathering her hair into a neat ponytail. That kept it off her face while she was working and, more important, while she was cooking or baking.

Buttoning her sweater against the morning chill, she came down for breakfast to find the main room of the Lutz house a scene of controlled chaos. The great-grandchildren were there with their mothers, selecting from a long row of ice skates that had been set out this morning. Meg noted every type of skate, from beginners' runners that attached directly to shoes to adult heavy black skates for hockey and racing, most of them well worn from years of being used and, no doubt, handed down. The younger Lutz children rushed in and out, balancing the completion of their chores with locating appropriately fitting skates for themselves. Meg noticed about a dozen hockey sticks stacked against the wall and a pile of thick black gloves on the bench.

James and the children were sitting off to one corner, also trying on skates.

"Hey, guys," Meg said as she came over.

"They invited us to skate with them," Sam said. "There's a pond that'll be ice! I've never done that before."

Lizzie was lacing up a pair of old but serviceable white skates. "You want to come, Mom?"

Meg hesitated. "Is Catherine going? Or any of the other women?"

"No," James answered. "They said they had too much to do. It's just dads and kids, I guess. We may get to play some hockey with them, too."

Meg already knew there would be a lot of work going on that day. Saturday was the regular cleaning day in the house, and the big event was on Tuesday. If the other women were staying behind, she would do the same.

"I'll stay here this morning," she said. "Maybe later I'll have a chance to get out and mess around with everybody."

James had moved to kneel in front of Sam and help tighten his laces. "Okay, these are good." He gave a couple of solid pats to the black skates before turning to Will. "How is it going?"

Will shook his head as he yanked off a skate. "Kinda tight." Clutching the skate in question, he got up to check out his other options. Seeing they didn't need her, Meg went back toward the kitchen area. Barbara stood at the table, a group of kerosene lamps gathered from around the house spread out before her. She was carefully cleaning them with a rag. Meg greeted her and, reaching into a cabinet for a mug, asked if she could assist.

"No, thank you. But my mother is at the root cellar, getting some food to cook for today and tomorrow. Maybe she needs help. The front walk is shoveled, but I don't know about the back . . ."

Meg, nodding, filled her cup with coffee. Practically hidden from view, she observed Jonathan and Eli hurry into the room, yanking on jackets and gloves before grabbing skates, hockey sticks, and hats. Several teenage boys in coats and black mufflers came to the front door, entering the house just long enough to pick out hockey sticks.

"Later," Barbara said to Meg, "we can go for a sleigh ride or be outside with the children, if you like."

Sam came running up to Meg to say goodbye. "It's so cool the way people come into each other's houses, isn't it? Everything's just right there, all together." He gave her a hug. "Bye. See you later."

"Have fun," she called out to her family.

James gave her a wave and a smile. Her older son and daughter also called out their goodbyes,

Lizzie applying the lip balm she always kept in her jacket pocket as she left.

A sliced loaf of banana bread had been set out on a plate on the counter, although most of it was already gone. Meg reached for a piece and took a bite. On a Saturday at home in Charlotte, she reflected, James would have been at the office or in his study working. If the kids had a free day, she would be the one taking them skating at an indoor rink, assuming she could have gotten them to agree to go in the first place, which was unlikely. Even so, she would have to drag Lizzie and Will practically by force. And it wouldn't have been happening until well after noon, when they might be willing to get out of their pajamas and into clothes.

"Are David and Samuel going skating, too?" she asked Barbara.

"No, they're cleaning out the barn now. Aaron already cleaned the chicken coop, so he left, but they have a lot of work. And tomorrow is a church Sunday. They want to finish things."

Meg was confused. "Don't you go to church every Sunday?"

Barbara shook her head. "No, every other Sunday."

"Oh." Surprised, Meg finished her coffee and rinsed out the cup. "Well, I'm going downstairs to see if I can help your mother. Then I'll shovel in the back."

Barbara nodded, her attention on a spot on one of the lamps that was giving her difficulty. She rubbed at it furiously.

Meg rotated her shoulders in small circles as she walked, wanting to loosen them up a bit as she went to help Catherine lift the enormous sacks in the cellar. Who needs free weights when you have beets and potatoes, she thought with a smile.

Everyone returned in time for lunch, the children ruddy-cheeked and in high spirits. James came over to kiss Meg hello on the cheek, cheerfully complaining that he had used muscles he didn't remember he even had, and would pay for it the next day. While she wasn't sure how friendly she wanted her response to him to be, she was genuinely pleased to see that the four of them had had a wonderful time together. James and Will discussed the fine points of their hockey game with the other participants during the entire first course of hot beef barley soup and bread. Lizzie, seated next to Meg, ate her entire bowl of soup without complaint as she told her mother how much she enjoyed the skating, even though so many kids had appeared throughout the course of the morning, she wouldn't have been surprised if the ice had opened up and they'd all fallen into the pond.

After lunch almost everyone headed back outside to play in the snow. This time Meg and the Lutz women bundled up and joined in. Snowball fights broke out everywhere, and children screamed with delight as they ducked. When sleighs began pulling up, the horses whinnying in the frosty air, the Hobarts were thrilled to find places amid the Lutz children and the neighbors offering the rides. Cuddling under blankets, her children and husband laughing beside her as they bounced along behind the trotting horses, Meg wondered why everyone in the world didn't want to take a sleigh ride every time it snowed. Rapt, she drank in the sights of the passing farms in their picture-perfect state, the deserted animal pens, their usual inhabitants inside the warm barns, and the gently rolling farmland, an endless narrow strip against the overwhelming expanse of the after-noon sky.

She glanced over to see James and Lizzie, their heads close together, looking out at something far away, James's arm outstretched as he pointed. The two of them engaged in conversation: That was something she couldn't recall seeing in ages.

"Is this not the greatest treat in the world?" she asked Will, who was sitting next to her.

"It's pretty awesome, I gotta admit," he answered, his eyes wide open and clear, his expression one of pure happiness.

She put an arm around him. He didn't pull away.

By the time evening rolled around, everyone was exhausted. After dinner most of the children settled down to board games, accompanied by snacks of pretzels and roasted marshmallows. Meg found herself seated at the table with Catherine and Barbara, who explained that they were going over seating details for the unmarried teenagers at the evening supper. Meg wanted to know more but refrained from interrupting them with what she guessed seemed like her endless questions.

During a momentary lull, she decided to jump in with a request she had been pondering for the past few hours. "I truly don't want to add to the things you have to deal with," she started, "but I wonder if you would do me a favor."

Both women looked at her as she chose her words.

"Every Christmas I bake my special brownies and oatmeal cookies. I've been doing it forever, and it kind of makes it Christmas for us. Would you do me the favor of letting me bake them for your wedding, Barbara? I promise I won't disappoint you—I really think your guests will like them."

Barbara smiled. "That's a wonderful thing you're offering to do."

"It would mean so much to me, for so many

reasons," Meg said. "But it would be my little contribution to wishing you a happy marriage."

"Thank you. I would be honored."

Meg laughed. "I'm not sure you should be honored. I don't know if they're *that* good."

"We'll see, won't we?" Catherine grinned. "On Monday we will add them with other baking that is still to do."

"Thank you. Thank you so much."

The two women had no idea of the significance it had for her, Meg thought. She hadn't missed a year since Lizzie was born. All three of her children adored the very fudgy brownies and the oatmeal cookies shot through with cranberries. It would have been unbearably sad for her to see the holiday come and go without them. Of course, Meg expected that they would be at her parents' house when the actual holiday rolled around. That was exactly why she needed to bake them before they left here. She knew perfectly well her parents weren't going to be excited about the cost, the mess, or the idea of letting their grandchildren run amok by eating all the brownies and cookies they wanted until they had run out.

That was the whole point, though, in Meg's view. What made it fun was the seemingly inexhaustible supply of sweets without—just this one time in the year—limits applied. Breakfast, lunch, or dinner, if you wanted brownies or cookies, you could have them. It wasn't such a big deal, considering they were gone in about three days, everyone satiated to the point of nausea, wanting nothing more to do with them until the next year.

Meg went to bed that night feeling that she had done her best to salvage a little bit of home for her family.

The next morning she got up to see the Lutzes leaving for worship, dressed in what must have literally been their Sunday best, black clothes that were basically the same style but not the same garments they wore during the workweek. They hadn't invited the Hobarts to go with them, and Meg and James sensed that it wasn't appropriate to ask.

Once all five of them had made it to the kitchen, they took seats around the table in the dim morning light to eat the breakfast Catherine had left for them. The dogs settled beneath the table, Racer snoring lightly, Rufus sitting at attention in case someone should drop a piece of food. Sam scratched the puppy's head.

Suddenly the five of them felt awkward in the silent house. Sam broke the silence first. "Old Samuel told me about their church service," he offered as he poured himself a bowl of cereal.

"You are so weird, spending all your time with that old man," Will said, although he was still too sleepy to put much energy into the insult. He took a long gulp from his glass of orange juice.

"I don't spend all my time with him," Sam answered in annoyance. "But at least I know stuff, and you don't, stupid."

"Oh, big expert over there," Will said with disdain.

"Let me guess," Lizzie broke in. "Their church service is twelve hours. Then there's a five-minute break, and they go back for another twelve hours."

Sam made a face at her. "No. I just know that it's always in somebody's house or barn, a different place all the time. They have, like, these benches they take around. The men and women sit separate. There's this book with all their songs and stuff that they've been using for, like, four hundred years."

"Sam, that's really interesting," James said, helping himself to some buttermilk pancakes, golden but, by now, cold. "Thanks for telling us."

"You're very welcome," Sam said primly before sticking out his tongue at Will. "Some of us prefer not to be ignorant."

"Some of us prefer not to be obnoxious little freaks," Will retorted, reaching for the pitcher of maple syrup.

"I wonder what time they'll get back," Meg said.

"They eat and hang around after," Sam informed her.

At the unexpected sound of the door opening, all five of them turned. Racer jumped to his feet and tore over to the door, barking wildly, startling them with his ability to run, much less move that fast. The puppy took off after him, loudly yapping.

A tall young man stepped inside. He was wearing blue jeans, work boots, and a plaid flannel shirt beneath an open quilted down jacket and a navy-blue knitted cap. In one hand he held a knapsack that he let drop to the floor. The two dogs were jumping and barking for his attention.

Clearly shocked, he stared at the people sitting around the table. "Who the heck are you?" he demanded.

James drew himself up in his chair as if positioning himself in case he had to confront this intruder. Meg's gaze was drawn to the boy's blue eyes.

"Excuse me, but we're guests here—" James started. As James spoke, the boy tugged off his cap, revealing a thatch of blond hair.

Of course, Meg realized. She put a hand on James's arm. "Wait."

Her husband stopped and looked at her.

Meg stood up and smiled at the boy. "You must be Benjamin. I'm *so* glad to meet you."

Chapter 13

By eleven o'clock on Monday morning, Meg couldn't decide which was more impressive: the amount of work being done by the dozen or so couples who had appeared at the Lutz house early that morning, or the calm and organized way in which they went about it. One couple, relatives of David Lutz, had been designated to oversee the entire operation, but, once assigned a task, everyone seemed to know exactly what to do. The members of the community had done this many times before, Meg reflected, but their efficiency was nonetheless startling.

The men had their own list of chores, and Meg couldn't resist sneaking out of the baking in Catherine's kitchen for a few moments to see the activity going on in Joseph's barn. She paused just inside the doorway to watch a small group assemble temporary long tables, rigging benches to table height and covering them with white cloths. Several men gathered around what appeared to be a floor plan of the seating, consulting on the arrangement of tables.

At that moment, Catherine's daughter Annie passed by and stopped to tap Meg on the shoulder. Guiltily, Meg jumped and turned around. "I know, I'm slacking off," she said, surprised to feel her face turning pink. "I'm sorry."

"It's okay." Annie laughed. "You are curious." She peered inside. "Okay. Over there, see where the tables meet to make like a letter L? That's the *Eck*, the corner place where you can see them best, where Barbara and Moses sit with the people in the wedding party." Annie pointed to a group of men in a different area, assembling and sorting huge quantities of food. "That is to make the bread stuffing that goes with the chickens. A *lot* of chickens."

"Where is all this cooking being done?" Meg asked. "There's not enough room in our three kitchens."

"Many houses. My father is now at a neighbor's barn to kill the chickens and prepare them for roasting, and my grandparents are chopping celery at a different house. I'm going back to my house, where we are peeling potatoes." Annie laughed. "It is quite a job, making mashed potatoes for three hundred people. Be glad you are not doing the mashing part."

Meg's eyes widened. "I hadn't thought about that. Wow."

"We have many other people making gravy and tapioca pudding, things like that. As much as possible, we cooked all this week, too. We rented propane stoves to set up in a tent here. We spread the work out tomorrow, too, so everybody has some time to enjoy themselves, right? First, most important, are the church service and the wedding vows. Then the celebration. It's the beginning of a new family, so it's a very happy day. And we have always done it exactly the same way."

Annie smiled and walked off. Meg watched her, thinking about what the young woman had just said. This marriage was truly about celebrating a union. They followed their traditions to bring a new Amish family into being. Anything else was outside the realm of what was important. Nobody had to compete with anybody. She had to laugh, thinking of the vast sums of money spent on some of the weddings she and James had attended over the years, most of it for the sole purpose of impressing.

As she headed back toward the Lutz house, she briefly pondered if it was truly possible to eliminate all desire to show off, even the tiniest bit. Several times she had heard the Lutzes talk disapprovingly about something or other being prideful or vain. They worked hard to avoid that.

Meg looked down as she crossed the road to make sure she didn't slip on the ice. When she happened to glance up, she saw the figures of her sons following behind Aaron, Eli, and Jonathan with their newly returned brother, Benjamin. All six carried what obviously were heavy buckets, the older boys straining under the weightiest loads. They deposited them by the back door at Annie's house, closest to her kitchen, and set off back to Cathcrine's. Will and Sam lagged behind, talking; Meg could see the younger Lutz boys engaged in animated conversation with Benjamin, practically jumping to get his attention. She smiled. The two boys reminded her of Racer and Rufus when Benjamin had appeared at the house yesterday morning. Jonathan, the elder brother, seemed to be keeping his distance. Benjamin was wearing Amish clothes today, but his hair-cut, trimmed relatively short and without the ubiquitous bangs sported by the other Amish men, made him stand out. Meg guessed the change in clothes was a sign of respect for his family, although the tension between Benjamin and his parents bubbled painfully close to the surface.

Meg had noticed that, as warm and friendly as they were, the adults of the Lutz clan were not particularly affectionate, at least not in front of her, with the one definite exception of how they treated the young children. Babies and toddlers got plenty of hugs and kisses. But she couldn't recall seeing the adults exchange a hug or a kiss or even an unnecessary touch. Perhaps they considered that private, not something for public display, or it just wasn't their way. Meg had no idea and was hardly going to ask. Even so, she was taken aback to see the cool greeting Benjamin received from his father and grandparents when they returned from their church service and found him at home. Maybe it had something to do with his indecision about his future. While warmer, Catherine had refrained from any big display of emotion, although Meg could see both joy and anguish on her face at the sight of her long-absent son.

Initially, the adults hadn't asked Benjamin where he had been or what he had been up to. The younger children, however, couldn't wait to hear about his escapades and hustled him off to another part of the house where they could have him all to themselves. He seemed only too glad to leave the room. Walking along now, watching the group of boys, Meg pondered the difficulty of Benjamin's choices. All she knew for sure, she reflected, was that the lives of these people were infinitely more complex than she understood.

By late afternoon, Meg was exhausted from the day's labors, but she never would have admitted it. Everyone around her was still going at full steam. One of the older women came over to inform her that she could start on her brownies and cookies. Meg was gratified that they had in fact set aside time for her. She had begun to think she would have to get up in the dead of night if she wanted a chance at her own baking.

James had purchased the supplies, only too glad they could contribute something to the celebration, however small. After sending little Rachel to find Lizzie, Meg began to assemble her ingredients. The goal was four hundred brownies and three hundred cookies. Just a tad more than the usual Christmas batch, she laughed to herself, but hey, this is the land of the Amish. They can do everything, and maybe, as long as I'm here, I can, too.

When Lizzie came running into the house behind Rachel, she was red-faced and out of breath. "What's wrong, Mom? Rachel said . . ." Lizzie trailed off as she saw the familiar baking ingredients. Her face broke into a wide grin. "Oh, Mom." She sighed with pleasure. "The brownies. And the oatmeal cookies, too? You're awesome."

Meg smiled at her. "Only if I can get some help. We need to make enough to feed a small city. So wash your hands and tie your hair back."

Lizzie didn't have to be told twice. "One sec, I'll be right there," she called out as she dashed toward the sink.

Meg was happy to see her daughter so excited. Her daughter's obvious longing for something familiar didn't escape her. Even when they left here, though, they weren't going back home, only on to another unfamiliar world. It would be soon, too. Just another few days, according to the mechanic.

Meg smoothed down the front of her borrowed apron. Then she moved forward, assessing what it would take to lift the enormous sack of flour before her.

When she and Lizzie finished arranging the last platter of brownies, both of them breathed sighs of vast relief. The desserts had come out just right, though they had never before attempted to bake them in such huge quantities. Catherine tasted a brownie and a cookie, giving a brisk nod and pronouncing them good in a definite tone of voice. This, Meg knew, was high praise. After the last pan was washed and put away, she and her daughter shared a high five and a long, tight hug.

By the time she got ready to head upstairs for the night, Meg felt that if she couldn't partake in any other part of the wedding celebration, she would be grateful for what she had already been allowed to see and do on this day. Just the time spent baking with Lizzie had been a supreme treat. She tried not to compare the obviously tight bonds of these people with the ephemeral connections of her own past. It made for a very sorry assessment of what passed for relationships. To be fair, she reminded herself, most of these people were related in some way. They spent all their lives together. And they had their own problems with one another. Yet Meg could see that the bonds of their religion and community overrode all other considerations.

After an incredibly long day, the huge but relaxed crowd of workers sat down to a supper infused with goodwill and laughter. They truly lived by the adage that work was its own reward, Meg reflected. Seated at the table, looking at the open, kind faces around her, she knew she would remember this day for a long time to come.

By the time she said her good nights, Meg was so tired, she wanted nothing more than to feel the pillow beneath her head. On her way down the hall, she passed the door to Benjamin's room, which was slightly open. When the boy had returned home, he'd kindly allowed Will to continue to stay in the room with him, while Sam moved in with Aaron. As Meg went by, she heard Benjamin say something and Lizzie and Will laugh in response. Guiltily, she paused to find out what they were discussing. She had no idea what her children talked about with the Lutz children, and the opportunity to find out was irresistible.

"No Christmas tree or lights or anything?" Will was asking in disbelief.

"No Santa Claus, none of that," Benjamin said. "We just hang out, have a big family meal, a couple of small presents. Nothing big, and mostly stuff you can use. The next day we go to worship."

"The next day?" Will asked. "The day *after* Christmas?"

"Yup."

"Can't get much different from that back where we live I mean lived," Lizzie said. "People have huge trees. Tons of presents. A lot of kids in my class would be away on vacation this week in Europe or, like, on a safari in Africa or something."

"Hart Jenkins was going to Cabo," Will said. "He goes every year with his parents and his grandparents."

"I've never heard of Cabo. Where is it?" Benjamin asked.

There was a momentary silence. "I don't totally know where it *is,*" Will said as offhandedly as he could manage to cover his ignorance. "But it's hot, and tons of people go there."

"The people who stay home go to a lot of parties," Lizzie put in. "That's what I'd be doing if we were home. Will, remember last year, when Patricia Woods had to get her stomach pumped?"

"Oh, man, that was nuts." Will sounded gleeful. His tone changed as he explained the situation to Benjamin. "She was a senior, but everybody heard about it, even in my school."

Lizzie picked up the story. "The assistant principal's son had a New Year's Eve party because his parents were away. She got so drunk, she hurled all over their white couch. Then she said she felt better, so she drank some more. She totally passed out, and they had to take her to the hospital to get her stomach pumped. She almost *died,* no kidding. They said, like, another twenty minutes and that would have been it.

"People at the party were so freaked." Lizzie's voice rose slightly in her excitement to share the icing on the cake. "Her friends who drove her to the hospital actually left her outside the emergency room and took off. Left her right there on the ground."

There was a pause as if they all were considering this display of concern for the unconscious girl.

"Whatever," said Lizzie, sounding a bit chastised. "But don't you want to get out and see more of the world?"

"I've seen some of it, at least some of this country," Benjamin replied. "I traveled around."

"Oh, man," Will said, "why would you come back here if you didn't have to? You don't have anything here. It's been so long since I've been on my computer, I'll never catch up with what's going on."

"Yeah," Lizzie sneered. "Like what pathetic girl hooked up with your buddy Harry because he played her that insanely bad song." Again an explanation for Benjamin's sake. "This kid is in ninth grade, and he wrote this one pitiful song. He picks a girl and tells her he wrote it just for her. He can't even, like, play the guitar, but he does this little serenade thing, and the girls fall for it every time. It's so disgusting!"

"Come on," said Will. "It's pretty brilliant, you gotta admit. Or it was until enough girls found out about it. They really ganged up on him. None of them will even talk to him anymore."

"Serves him right. I mean, they're stupid, but at least they're not *that* stupid," Lizzie retorted. "But yeah, about not talking, I wonder what happened with Suki and Michelle."

"You mean those skanky girls you hang out with, with the insanely straight hair? The ones with all those jangly bracelets and crap?" Will asked.

"They're not skanky, and they have their hair straightened with this process that everybody does. It looks great, for your information."

Will snorted. "If you say so."

Lizzie deigned to continue. "The point is, they went on this hike together, and when they came back they weren't speaking. They won't tell anybody what happened." She paused. "I'm kind of happy I don't have to deal with that anymore. Everybody had to take sides. It was hard, because we didn't even know what they were so mad about. But it was getting really ugly."

Meg leaned against the hallway wall. This

was the first time she had heard any of these stories. It appears I know absolutely nothing about the lives my children have been leading, she thought.

Lizzie went on, her tone more reflective. "I have to admit, it's been pretty great to be away from all that. It was totally getting to me. You guys here definitely don't have the stress of the social stuff."

"One thing is," Will said, "it was kind of boring at home. I mean, everybody's on the computer or their phone all the time, and you have to do that or you're just out of things. I didn't used to think that, but now I kinda do. At first I thought it was insanely boring here, but there's really something to do all the time. I miss basketball, but you do lots of other sports and outside stuff. There's nothing to do at home, ever."

"Yeah, and I like the feeling of having done something you can see and touch, you know?" Lizzie added. "Maybe that sounds stupid. I mean, there's way too much work here. It's ridiculous. But it's nice to *do* something. Does that make any sense?"

"It's kind of like there's nothing to do here *but* work and then get a little break," Will reflected. "But when you get to play, it's like you earned it."

Meg was practically holding her breath, hanging on every word.

"So when do you decide what you're going to do about leaving or not?" Lizzie asked.

As Benjamin spoke, Meg realized he had virtually no trace of the family accent—perhaps, she thought, because he had spent the most time living among outsiders.

"I liked a lot of what I saw while I was traveling. I had a bunch of jobs, met a lot of people. It was all really interesting. I love music, and I'm going to miss that. I also really liked driving a car, and TV and movies. And the computer, of course."

His bed squeaked; Meg could tell he had stood up and was moving around the room.

"But it's all the stuff you're talking about. I met really nice people, but I saw that people can also be rotten. And lonely. And a lot of things I don't like and don't want to be. Besides, it would be really hard on my parents if I left. There's also a girl here that I missed." His tone turned severe. "You tell anybody about her, and you'll be in big trouble."

"Okay, okay," Will said. "No problem."

Benjamin went on. "So I've already decided that I'm coming back. After Christmas, I'll go finish up some things, and then I'm moving back for good."

Meg inhaled sharply. He had made up his mind. He was returning for good. She wanted to jump up and down with happiness for Catherine and David.

"Did you tell anybody yet?" Lizzie wanted to know.

"I'm waiting until after the wedding. It's not a time to draw attention to myself."

No, no, no, Meg implored him silently, it's okay to draw attention to yourself this time. Don't torture your parents anymore. Don't torture *me* by making me keep that from them.

Will spoke with exaggerated seriousness. "Your secret's safe with us."

"Thank you, my man," Benjamin said, laughing.

The three of them continued to talk, but Meg hurried down the hall to her own room. She was grateful for all she had learned from her eavesdropping. Thinking back on the many times she had told her children that it was absolutely wrong to eavesdrop, she fervently hoped they would never find out about it.

On the morning of the wedding itself, the atmosphere in the house turned more serious. Everyone left for a worship service at nine. It was expected to last about three hours, with the actual wedding vows taking place near the end. Meg felt an almost maternal thrill at seeing Barbara go off in her new white cape and apron over a dark-blue dress, the same color worn by the girls who were her attendants. Having been told that the bride and groom wore new clothes, Meg knew there were other differences from their regular Sunday clothes, but she wasn't knowledgeable enough to discern the subtleties.

Other non-Amish friends of the families were among the invited guests; they had been asked to arrive at eleven o'clock, closer to when the wedding vows began. Much to the surprise of Meg and James, David and Catherine stayed at the house for most of the morning as well. The Hobarts remained behind the entire time, helping others get ready to serve the luncheon meal. Just before guests were due to appear, they retreated to their rooms to change into whatever clothing they had with them that might be appropriate. None of them had packed anything resembling party clothes, but the casual clothes they did have, washed and neatly pressed, felt better suited to the occasion of cooking and serving.

All at once, it seemed, dozens of buggies pulled up to Joseph's house, guests spilling out into the cold. As she retied her hair into a neat ponytail, Meg watched from her bedroom window. It was such an incredible sight, she thought, all those buggies pulled by horses, truly like stepping back in time. She noted a line of cars parked nearby as well, no doubt transporting the English guests.

"Okay," James said, coming up behind her to glance out the window. "This is really going to be something. Let's go."

Meg turned to look at him. Gone was the furrowed brow she had seen for months, the pursed lips and angry expression. He appeared healthy and relaxed. She followed him out of the room.

"C'mon, everybody, let's get going," she called out to her children as she hurried down the stairs. They, too, had assignments for the day, from keeping water glasses filled to collecting dirty dishes. Grabbing their coats from the wall of hooks, she and James practically ran across to Joseph's barn to reach the tented-off workspace containing the propane stoves.

Meg and James watched from what felt like backstage as Barbara and Moses took their places at the central location of the *Eck*, the bride to the left of the groom, attendants and young relatives seated nearby. Girls and boys filed in, sitting apart. Today, Catherine had explained to Meg, the new couple's aunts and uncles had the honor of tending to the needs of all those in this area of the reception.

Meg soaked up the sights and sounds. She was intrigued by the numerous vases and jars containing celery that ran down the length of the tables like floral centerpieces, apparently a long-standing tradition. Most guests hadn't brought gifts to the wedding, but many of the English guests, or relatives from far away, had, and the presents were set aside in a small display; she noted the assortment of useful items ranging from roasting pans to a chain saw. Those working in the kitchens somehow knew the correct order in which a seemingly endless parade of food was to be presented, and Meg heaped hot food onto platter after platter, not just the chicken and bread stuffing dish but hams, ducks, the infamous mashed potatoes, creamed celery, noodles, salads, casseroles, pickled beets with eggs, coleslaw, bread and butter, fruit, pudding, and ice cream. She was stunned by the sheer number of cakes and sweets set out.

Toward the end of the meal, she couldn't resist going to check on how her brownies and cookies were faring with the crowd—and was relieved to see that the guests had found room for them. Judging by the rate at which they disappeared, Meg noted, they must have met with everyone's satisfaction. Abashed, she reminded herself that she was experiencing a decidedly un-Amish moment of pride.

The closest relatives, including David and Catherine, took their meal at a table in the kitchen. Teenagers and younger guests were done first and then left the dining area. When all the guests had finished, it was two-thirty, time for an afternoon sing. Meg was pleased to recognize the doctor who had treated her and James the night they had arrived at the Lutzes', and she went over to thank him again for his help. They talked while some of the adults attempted to round up the teenage guests from wherever they had scattered, although Meg could see many of them remained elusive, including her own. She noticed Sam standing with Aaron and another boy, but there was no sign of Lizzie or Will. In the back of her mind, she wondered if she should check on them, but first one and then another distraction drew her attention. When the singing got under way, she was glad for the opportunity to sit down. She knew she would be helping to serve another meal later in the day. Annie had explained that the younger guests would stay for supper and the celebration would continue until very late.

The day was progressing like a lovely, slow-moving dream. The sensation was shattered when she saw Will run into the barn, crying, blood smeared around a large cut on his chin. Wild-eyed, he looked around.

Meg jumped up and ran over, the people seated close to her turning to see what was wrong.

"Will, what is it?" Meg wrapped an arm around his shoulder, hustling him outside the barn, away from the guests, as she smoothed back his hair so she could get a better look at his injuries. "What happened? Where are you hurt?"

"It's not me." Will was crying harder, having difficulty getting out his words. "Amanda. I think she broke something."

"What? What are you talking about? Where is she?" Meg took his chin in her hand, forcing him to look her directly in the eyes. "Tell me."

"It's—It was stupid, and I'm really sorry." Will wiped his running nose with his jacket sleeve, his face growing redder as the tears came in full force.

Meg's voice rose. "Where is Amanda? Is she okay?"

"Lizzie's with her back there, on the road." He pointed in some general direction as he tried to catch his breath. "The buggy turned over. Going t-too fast. She can't walk now."

"*What?* Oh, Will, oh no!" Meg turned, grabbing his hand. "We have to get Catherine."

"No, don't tell her," Will wailed. "She'll be mad."

Meg had already started running toward the tent where she had last seen Catherine. "Hurry."

They found her talking with a group of women, but she broke away when she saw a frantic Meg approaching with her son in tow.

"Tell her," Meg commanded Will as they got closer.

"I'm so, so sorry," Will began, words tumbling out of his mouth. "The buggy fell over. Amanda got hurt, maybe broke her leg. Lizzie's with her. They're on the side of the road, it's not far. But Amanda can't walk at all."

Catherine's expression didn't change. She nodded and quickly moved past them. "Come with me. You will show us."

Meg kept Will off to the side, hoping they would be less disruptive, and watched Catherine make a beeline for a gray-haired non-Amish woman in a pale-green silk dress at one of the tables. Catherine bent over, whispered in her ear, and the woman rose to her feet, smiling and saying a few quick words to the guests she had been seated with. The woman grabbed her coat and headed toward the exit with Catherine. Meg and Will hurried to catch up, and the four of them headed to a parked car.

Catherine looked around to make sure Will was coming and got in on the passenger side. Meg realized that Catherine might not be allowed to drive a car, but she was allowed to be a passenger in one, and it was a lot faster to get to her daughter in a car than a buggy. Meg and Will practically dove into the backseat as the woman pulled onto the road.

"Will," Catherine said calmly, "say where."

"Just up there, you make a left turn." His voice was shaky. "It was when we went around that corner, the whole thing fell over."

"Is Amanda awake? Can she talk?"

"Oh yes, yes, it's nothing like that," Will rushed to reassure Catherine.

She expelled a small breath and turned to

face them in the back. "This is my friend Nina Moore. She can take Amanda to the hospital if we need, so that is good."

Will let out a small, tremulous sob. "I'm really sorry. It was my fault. I know I shouldn't have touched the reins."

Meg stared at him. "Touched the reins? What do you mean?"

"We, we . . . Lizzie and me, we were gonna deliver stuff with Amanda and Jonathan," he started miserably.

"The pies," Catherine said. "Jonathan and Amanda had to take pies to King's. The regular delivery."

Meg was startled to think the two would leave their sister's wedding to make a delivery. Then it occurred to her that it was a Tuesday, so businesses would be operating as usual. The Lutz family had a delivery to make, so they would make it, wedding or not.

"Go on," she said brusquely to her son.

He seemed to shrink in his seat. "Amanda and Lizzie were in back, and I was sitting in the front. Jonathan was gonna drive, but then he had to go back inside to talk to somebody for a second. So Lizzie was teasing me. You know how she can be." He looked for sympathy in his mother's eyes but found none. "She was daring me to drive the buggy, saying, like, even Aaron could do it, stuff like that." He paused to wipe his face with his jacket sleeve. "All I did was pick up the reins a little, and the horse just started going. I didn't do *anything,* I swear. We were having fun, really, it was okay. Amanda said to stop, but you know, for a minute I was really driving. Then the horse started going too fast, and I couldn't get him to stop. It was scary." Fresh tears filled his eyes.

"What happened next?" Catherine asked.

"When we came to this corner, I didn't tell it to, but the horse just turned really fast. The whole thing tipped over. Everybody screamed, but Amanda couldn't get up." His voice got very small. "So I ran back. That's it."

For the first time, Meg heard Nina speak: "Here they are." She pulled over, and all of them got out. Meg caught her breath at the sight before her. The horse stood upright, still partially connected to the rig, which Meg recognized at once as Jonathan's buggy. It lay on its side, badly damaged, the rear wheel shattered. Smashed pies and boxes were strewn everywhere, the snow smeared with pieces of crust, apple filling, and chocolate. Just past the mess, sitting on a blanket, Lizzie had a protective arm around Amanda, who was rocking back and forth, her leg extended in front of her. Lizzie's terrified expression turned to naked relief when she saw the women emerge from the car.

In an instant, Catherine was kneeling beside

her daughter, softly asking questions. Amanda winced as Catherine lightly touched her leg, trying to determine the extent of the injury. When Lizzie and Catherine moved to help her up, Amanda cried out in pain before even attempting to put any weight on her foot.

Nina Moore was standing next to Meg and Will, watching. "That leg very well may be fractured. We'll go straight to the hospital."

Meg was amazed by Amanda's stoicism. Although pale, she stood uncomplaining, leaning against Lizzie and Catherine, while Nina brought the car as close as she could and they helped her maneuver into the back. Then Lizzie came over to join her mother and brother.

Meg made a quick decision. She turned to her children. "I'm going to the hospital. One of you stay here with the horse, and one of you run and find Jonathan. Tell him about his buggy. Ask him how you should clean up the mess and who can help you. When I get back, there shouldn't be any trace of this food left."

She headed back to the car. Catherine had climbed in the back beside her daughter, whose silence belied the pain in her eyes.

"Mom—" Lizzie called after her own mother, but Meg yanked open the car door.

"Just go," she said.

At the hospital, Nina and Meg took a seat in the waiting area while Catherine followed her daughter through the inner double doors to the emergency room for an X-ray.

"Well," Nina said, "this has turned out to be an even busier day than anyone could have guessed."

Meg shook her head. "I don't know if I'm more angry or embarrassed. My kids have done a lot of things I'm not too proud of since we've been staying here, but this . . ."

"I heard about you being here. You and David almost crashing into each other. The Lutzes are a wonderful family, aren't they? You got very lucky when you wound up in their house."

Meg smiled. "Yes, but we only wound up there because we nearly killed David Lutz. Not so lucky for him."

Nina smiled back at her. "But you didn't kill him. Instead, you made friends with him."

"That's a very nice way to put it." Meg felt grateful to her.

"Happily, it all worked out."

Meg grew serious. "I'd like to know how this is going to work out. Let's see: My kids have injured Amanda, destroyed Jonathan's buggy, and disrupted Barbara's wedding. Oh, and wait —last but not least, they ruined the entire restaurant order, which means the family lost that money altogether. All because of their completely thoughtless behavior. It's not as if they don't know better."

"Take it easy," Nina said. "It'll be okay."

"You don't know how incredible these people have been to us," Meg said. "They're the last people on earth I'd want to cause trouble for. And to hurt one of their children—I can't bear it."

The other woman put a comforting hand on Meg's. "Look, if you know them, you know they're very understanding. Nobody was seriously hurt. That's what matters."

Meg sighed.

Catherine pushed open one of the double doors and walked over to them. "Her leg is broken, but it's not such a bad break. They have to put on a cast. We'll be here for a while. You two go back and enjoy the rest of the wedding."

"No, Catherine, don't be silly," Nina said. "We'll wait."

"Of course," said Meg.

"There is no reason for you to sit here. Go back."

Meg shook her head firmly. "Absolutely not."

Catherine looked at her and saw she would not be dissuaded. "If you wish." She turned to go back to her daughter.

Meg and Nina spent the next hour talking about what it had been like for the Hobarts to experience life on the Lutz farm. Meg was thrilled to be able to discuss some of what she had observed with another non-Amish person who knew about their way of life. They talked about the wedding and all the traditions associated with it. Meg learned from Nina that Barbara and Moses would not go on a honeymoon. As Amanda had partly explained on the night all the women were quilting, they would do what was typical of newlyweds, spending weeks visiting their wedding guests, sometimes making multiple visits in one weekend or traveling far afield. That way they would be ready to get back to work in time for the spring planting.

Nina was so easy to talk to that Meg felt as if they were old friends. She found herself describing how she had loved baking with the women, the soothing rhythms of the work and the camaraderie. She explained what a privilege it was to be allowed to bake for the wedding meal. Laughing, she recalled her immense relief that multiplying the recipes for her brownies and cookies to feed hundreds of people had worked out.

At the mention of Meg's desserts, Nina's eyes lit up. "You made those? They were fantastic."

"Thank you so much."

"I was wondering where they came from. I assumed it was some distant relative because I've never had them at any of the local Amish functions. Well, the ones I've been invited to."

"I make them every year. My family likes them."

Nina leaned in closer to Meg. "You know, I run a small inn about twenty-five miles from here. Every afternoon we serve tea with some kind of biscuit or sweet. Would you consider baking me some brownies and some of those cookies? Or other cookies, if you've got any recipes you really love. Give me a price, and if it's reasonable, I'll get a few dozen of each, and we'll try it out. I love to serve things that people can't get anywhere else."

"Really?" Meg was so flattered, she didn't know what to say. "Are you serious?"

Nina regarded her with mild surprise. "Well, of course. Why not?"

Meg smiled. "Yes. Why not?"

Chapter 14

Meg approached Annie's house with dread. After yesterday's fiasco, she was as embarrassed as she could remember ever having been in her life. Her children, for whom she was responsible, had wreaked havoc on one of the Lutz family's most important occasions. She was also exhausted, which made her feel even less able to cope with her mortification. Too upset to sleep, when she finally did fall asleep, she was awakened in the middle of the night by what she assumed was a dream in which she heard people moving around downstairs. She kept dozing off only to wake again, thinking she'd heard voices.

In the morning she learned that she hadn't been dreaming at all. She had been hearing Barbara and Moses downstairs in the still-dark early morning, following another Amish tradition in which the bride and groom spend their wedding night at the bride's parents' house and get up especially early to clean the house. The idea intrigued Meg. So unlike the usual concept of a wedding night. Again, the tradition was about helping the community and each other, not just the individual.

All the early-dawn cleaning by Barbara and her new husband meant that the downstairs was spotless, but Meg had circles under her eyes and wanted only to crawl back into bed and hide. Amanda was stuck in the house with her leg in a cast, dependent on crutches to get anywhere. The buggy sat in pieces in the barn. And now the Lutz women had to congregate at Annie's to replace yesterday's entire order of pies. Miserable, Meg had dragged her feet for as long as she dared before coming over this morning.

"Mom, wait up."

Meg turned to see Lizzie running after her, sliding a bit on the icy ground. Meg had said little to her daughter or to Will since returning from the hospital yesterday.

Late last night, after they had all gotten back to the house, she had heard James yelling at them for a very long time. She decided that adding her own screaming recriminations wouldn't help matters. Whatever James had said, it must have gotten through to them, because when the children emerged from the room, they were pale and practically shaking with guilt.

Now Lizzie caught up to her mother, breathing hard. "I want to come with you. To help. I know you have to make the food all over again."

"Okay." Meg looked at her for a moment.

"It's strange, but I didn't even think to ask you to help." She shrugged.

Lizzie didn't reply, pursing her lips and looking down.

When they got to Annie's house, Meg hesitated before reaching for the doorknob. She was trying to prepare for the silent stares they would receive.

Inside the kitchen, it was a day like every other, the room fragrant and warm. Leah, Catherine, Annie, and Sue were combining the ingredients for apple and shoofly pies. They all glanced up at the appearance of Meg and her daughter, but their greetings were indistinguishable from those of any other time.

"Good, you are here," said Catherine, in the process of stirring batter in a large wooden bowl, "so you can measure the flour for the next batch."

Perhaps noticing Lizzie's fearful expression, Sue took the unusual step of handing her an apron instead of letting her retrieve one herself. "After you wash your hands, you can help me slice more apples," she told Lizzie. Her voice held only friendly politeness.

Leah offered Lizzie a knife. "Here, you use this one."

Meg almost sagged with relief. I could kiss these women, she thought. Even Leah is acting as if nothing has happened.

She stood next to Annie, who was taking a measuring cup to a large tub of butter.

"Can you replace everything from yesterday?" Meg asked.

Annie nodded. "We will make extra pies, but we talked to the store owner." She smiled. "He will take some of the cookies and pastries we have left from the wedding instead of twice as many pies today. He can't sell so many pies, but maybe he can sell pies and cookies. So everybody is happy."

That's one problem solved, Meg thought, thanks to the resourcefulness of these women.

When she found herself next to Catherine later, she tried to think what words might possibly help to make things right. She was unable to come up with any. Nonetheless, she couldn't pretend nothing had happened. "I'm so very sorry about—"

Catherine interrupted her. "Thank you. But you think I don't know how you are feeling about this? I see it on your face. Please don't be unhappy. You should not be. It was an accident, and nothing so terrible happened. Amanda's leg will be fine. Everything else can be fixed. It is not important."

"Oh, but it is important," Meg cried. "There's Amanda, and the wedding and the damage to the buggy—how can you ever forgive us?"

Catherine stopped what she was doing and

turned to look directly at Meg. "It is already forgiven. We believe in this very, very strongly. If we ourselves are to be forgiven, how could we not forgive someone else?"

Meg felt tears fill her eyes. "You're an amazing person," she said.

"No," Catherine said, "no more amazing than anyone else. I just follow what I believe, and it always leads me down the right path."

Meg felt an enormous weight being lifted from her shoulders. She resisted the impulse to hug Catherine.

Back at the Lutz house, Meg told James about the conversation. He shook his head. "These people are something else, aren't they?" he agreed. "Will came out to the barn to help repair the rig, and they were as nice to him as if he'd just stopped by to give them a hand instead of being the one who'd broken the darn thing. Frankly, I think their kindness has made him feel worse."

"I guess, in a weird way, it would probably be easier for the kids to deal with everyone being angry at them," Meg said thoughtfully. "They could shrug it off. They could whine about how they hadn't *meant* for anything to happen. You know"—in an exaggerated tone, she mimicked their indignant protests—" 'It was an *ac*cident. I'm *sorry,* okay?'"

James smiled at her impression.

"But no one's even asking for an apology," she went on, "so their usual ways of dealing with being in trouble won't work."

"Fiendishly clever," James said with a laugh. "The worst punishment of all."

"But it's not like the Lutzes even want to punish them," Meg protested.

"Among their own people, it's a whole different thing. But for our kids, it's like they're being killed with kindness."

"Well," said Meg, crossing her arms, "we certainly let them get out of control. I feel pretty responsible."

"Hey, I agree they've been pretty bratty here. But it's not so shocking that they would act up, given what they're going through."

"Does that justify what they pulled yesterday?"

He shook his head. "No, not at all. But let's watch what happens now that they're dealing with some real consequences for their behavior."

They watched what happened almost in disbelief. For the rest of the day, Lizzie was either doing Amanda's regular chores or sitting beside her, talking to her, fetching whatever she needed. Will was also busy all day, attempting to help on the rig repairs, then assisting the men who had come to dismantle the extension to the barn. The materials were going straight to the home where the next wedding was to be held.

Meg suspected the children's goodwill might

wear off by the next day, but on Thursday there was more of the same. Both children served, cleared, and cleaned up after breakfast without a word. Lizzie helped Amanda get to the table and waited on her, making conversation as if they were old friends. Will divided his attention equally among Eli, Aaron, and Sam, a shock in itself to his younger brother. Sam had heard the whole story, but he instinctively understood that it was not a subject he should bring up, much less tease his older siblings about. He acted as if it were nothing new for his brother and sister to be solicitous of him, an extremely wise move on his part, Meg thought.

Neither Lizzie nor Will showed the slightest sign that they were anything but sincere. Even better for them, no one in the Lutz households appeared to notice—or, in their usual kind way, chose not to notice—that anything was different. Meg and James were careful to follow their lead. They refrained from making any comment that might make Lizzie and Will retreat into a defensive posture.

To Meg, it was as if some invisible wall around her children had been knocked down, allowing them to drop their air of superiority and get on with the business of being themselves. Or rather, she corrected herself, their best selves. In fact, she realized, they weren't even arguing with each other anymore.

At one point, she passed the open door to Benjamin's bedroom and stopped to stare in amazement. Even though Benjamin was a little better than Will at cleaning up, there hadn't been much change in the condition of the room. Today Meg saw that, for the first time, Will had made his bed as if he were an army recruit, neat and tight. Everything on his side of the room had been put away, every surface was clean. When she went to look into Amanda's bedroom, she found more of the same, but the entire room had been gone over thoroughly. This could only have been done by Lizzie that morning, given Amanda's condition.

Every time Meg saw her daughter that day and the next, she was either working or attending to Amanda. At one point, Meg found the two girls relaxing on their beds, each with a book in her hand. She stuck her head in the room to ask if they wanted anything. Lizzie looked up over the top of her book to say thanks, they were fine. It was then that Meg saw that her daughter was three quarters of the way through *Tom Sawyer.* Meg had to turn away in a hurry so Lizzie wouldn't catch the smile on her face.

It was more of the same with Will: If he wasn't hard at work with his father or David, he was outside with Eli and his friends, walking through the snow-covered fields or running off to skate or play ice hockey.

Both her children initially steered clear of Jonathan, whose buggy they had wrecked, but quickly they saw that even he bore them no ill will.

When Meg decided it was time to take Nina up on her offer to buy some brownies, Lizzic was right there to help get them ready. Meg decided to bake a few different kinds of cookies along with the oatmeal-cranberry ones. She and Lizzie debated the merits of chocolate versus fruit fillings, and peanut butter flavoring versus coconut. Meg struggled to remember recipes she had made years and years before. They measured and mixed for hours, then watched over their creations, teasing each other about how often the other one wanted to open the oven doors to check. When the cookies came out golden brown, they celebrated with war whoops. As far as Meg was concerned, if that had been the end of the entire endeavor, it would have been well worth it just to have spent that afternoon laughing with her daughter again.

As it turned out, Nina picked up the food in person. She had wanted to stop by and see how Amanda's leg was faring. While she was there, she sampled one of everything and pronounced it all wonderful. Before she left, she requested a second, larger batch for the following week.

Catherine was delighted for Meg. "Now you will have your own business," she teased Meg as they cleared the table. "I will tell everyone that the master cookie baker got started here."

Meg laughed, but she was uncomfortable. Catherine had spoken the thought Meg herself had been too afraid even to voice. Day after day, watching those women turn out the endless pies, cakes, and breads, Meg saw that baking for a business was backbreaking work. Yet it could be done. The business required loving care and constant tending, but it was possible to maintain a small-scale operation. Somewhere in the back of her mind, it had occurred to her that perhaps she could do something like it on her own. But it was a thought she had refused to let herself develop.

Now, as Catherine voiced the idea, Meg's spirit lifted hearing her words. But almost as quickly she came up against the same obstacle that was in the way of everything else: She wouldn't be going back to her own home. She was going to be a guest in her parents' home, and they would never support such an endeavor.

Without support, both financial and personal, it would be unmanageable. Her parents didn't have the equipment, and they would never invest in any—that Meg knew without having to ask. What they *would* have was an endless list of reasons why the idea was doomed to fail. Now that she thought about it, she wondered what kind of customers she could come up with in a town like theirs, where specialized baked goods were not exactly in high demand.

No, she quickly realized, it was a pointless idea. She had no kitchen equipment, no money to pay for the initial supplies, no customers beyond Nina, and no prospects for any others.

She would have to figure out something else.

Chapter 15

The buggy approached the house, David Lutz and James barely visible inside. It was late afternoon, and they were returning from a trip to buy some farming supplies. In addition, they had checked on the progress of the Hobarts' car. Meg and Catherine sat on rocking chairs on the front porch, bundled up against the cold, enjoying a few minutes of quiet conversation before heading inside to start preparing supper.

The horse came to a stop just outside the barn. The men jumped out on opposite sides of the rig and hurried over to the two women.

"Wait until you hear this," James said.

Meg and Catherine looked up at him expectantly.

"The car will be ready in the morning."

David nodded in agreement. "Ready for the road and like new, the man said. You can pick it up tomorrow."

Meg sat up straight. "No! Are you serious?" She was so startled by the news, she realized she had actually stopped thinking this day would ever really come. Feeling her stomach drop, she also realized that she had come to hope it never would. Which made no sense. It's not as if we can stay with these people forever, she reprimanded herself. Sooner or later, we have to go back to reality—our reality, at least.

"They did a fantastic job, I saw that much," James went on. "It really does look like new."

Meg could only nod. The thought of the five of them piling back into that car and heading for the highway made her want to shudder.

James was watching her obvious distress. "We should get to your parents' house before Christmas Eve," he said, his tone hopeful.

It was a weak attempt to sound encouraging. They both knew the truth. Spending Christmas there was not an inducement to get going but, rather, something they would both prefer to avoid.

Catherine listened as she rocked in her chair. Meg glanced up in time to see Catherine lock eyes with her husband as something unspoken passed between them. David nodded almost imperceptibly.

"It is a very busy time on the roads now, right before Christmas," Catherine said as if she were mulling over travel conditions. "That is not so good." She paused. "Would you maybe stay with us a little longer? Then the roads will be safer."

"Wow. That's a wonderful offer," said James. "But we can't put you out any more than we already have. The roads will be okay. Remember, we'll be in a car."

"We all know your car is not safe," David said. "It tried to kill me."

"And it would be nice for all the children to have Christmas Day together," Catherine went on, as if no one had spoken. "I believe they would enjoy that, yes?"

Meg knew she should protest, say they had already stayed too long as it was. Yet those were not the words that came out of her mouth. "The children would enjoy it, and we would enjoy it, too." She looked at James. "I would like to stay. Wouldn't you?"

James smiled. "Of course I would." He turned to David. "If you're sure about this . . ."

"Yes, we are sure," David replied.

Catherine stood. "That is settled. Come, Meg, we will get some peaches from the basement for supper, and some beets."

Meg got up. She loved Catherine and David even more for the way they had handled the invitation. They were far too thoughtful to come out and flatly offer to rescue the Hobart family from what promised to be a dreary holiday. And Meg was touched beyond words that they wanted her family to share this holiday with theirs.

"James, you and I have to go see the chickens," David said, turning toward the coop. "Aaron tells me we have some wire to fix."

A little later, when Sam asked Meg permission to go to the store with Old Samuel and Leah, she saw an opportunity. She handed Sam some money and gave him instructions, then swore him to secrecy. Proud of the trust she was putting in him, and a little anxious about the responsibility, he told her she could count on him and went off to carry out his assignment.

After supper that night, the house was buzzing with activity. Lamplight cast a glow throughout the main room. The littlest Lutz children from next door and friends of varying ages made ornaments, simple stars and words that celebrated the religious meaning of the holiday. These, along with some pieces of greenery and pinecones, were the only decorations to be hung up.

Leah and Catherine sat at the table putting the final touches on the quilt that would be a holiday gift for Sarah, the schoolteacher. In the kitchen, Lizzie and eight-year-old Rachel made chocolate-dipped pretzels under the direction of Amanda, who sat nearby with her leg propped up on a chair. The enticing smell of melted chocolate permeated the air. Will and Sam played Monopoly with Eli and Aaron. Sam held Rufus the entire time, scratching the contented dog behind the ears. Annie dropped by to pick up all the youngest children and was delayed when her presence drew David and Old Samuel into the main room. Somehow, the greetings of the adults evolved into a session of storytelling for the children.

Meg and James found themselves at loose ends. Everyone around them was occupied. "Want to go get some air?" he asked her.

She nodded. Grabbing jackets, they headed out. It was bitingly cold.

"Freezing," James remarked. "Feels like it'll snow tonight."

Meg laughed. "You're beginning to sound like a farmer, speculating about the weather. Boy, that was something I don't think I ever heard you do in Charlotte."

At the mention of the city, they both fell silent. They stood on the porch, surveying the stars in the night sky.

"Charlotte feels very far away," James finally said. "Everything feels very far away." He moved off the porch, then turned to her. "The moon is pretty bright. Want to walk a bit?"

"Okay."

They set off toward the road.

When James spoke again, it was so hushed, Meg wasn't sure she heard him correctly. "I've never really apologized for what I did. I know that."

She didn't say anything, just kept walking, her eyes on the ground ahead of her.

"I guess," he went on, "I didn't know how to. But that's not an excuse."

"No, it isn't."

"I was so angry at myself. There was just no way a guy as smart as I am could be as stupid as that. I couldn't handle it."

There was another silence before James spoke again.

"The first problem was getting fired. It isn't the end of the world, I know that, but it was for me. In a million years—I was just *not* a guy who got fired. Impossible. Yeah, there were financial problems at the firm, things that had nothing to do with me, but we were in a bad position. Still, the ones who were getting laid off weren't gonna be me."

He didn't say anything for another few minutes. They walked along, ice and snow crunching beneath their boots.

He sighed. "It's hard to be the kind of jerk who can't handle life when he isn't the alpha dog anymore. That's what led to the next step and the next, until the whole thing exploded in my face."

"Not just in *your* face," Meg pointed out. "All of our faces."

"Yeah, that's the part I didn't get until it was too late." He shook his head. "But by then I couldn't admit what I'd done. Not even to myself."

"And now?"

"If we had gone straight to your parents' house, I really have to wonder if you and I would have made it. The tension between us was too much. I don't think we could have survived. But here, we've been removed from everything that defined us, good *and* bad. To tell you the truth, this feels like the first time I've been able to breathe in months—hell, in years."

Able to breathe, Meg thought. Exactly. Here, she was able to breathe again.

He stopped and turned to her. "I don't know if you'll forgive me or not. But I am sorry from the bottom of my heart. You have every right to leave me and every right to hate my guts. I understand that you don't trust me anymore. I wouldn't trust me, either. Frankly, I have no idea what it would take for me to win your trust back." He took a deep breath. "But I do want to win it back. I want us to go on together."

"I'm not sure I know what to say. I can't tell you, 'Okay, thanks for saying sorry, everything's fine again.' "

"I know."

"I'm not sure I *can* ever trust you again, or how you could make that happen. Right now I'm more worried about how we're going to survive, *literally* survive, once we leave here.

And going to live with my parents is a sorry answer to our problems. It's not an answer at all. The more I think about it, the worse I know it's going to be. It's not like we're nineteen and have to put up with staying in the basement for a few months. This is going to be a nightmare for all of us."

There was no need for him to comment. She knew he agreed with her.

"We'll be at each other's throats again in no time," she added.

"I wish I could come up with another solution." He kicked at a small rock in the road.

"For a minute there, I thought I had one," she said. "Remember the woman who drove us to the hospital when Amanda hurt her leg? She runs an inn, and she bought some of my brownies and cookies to serve to her customers. She really liked them."

James looked at her in surprise. "You're kidding! That's great. You didn't tell me that."

Her tone was wry. "Well, it's not like we're sharing a whole lot lately, is it? Anyway, Catherine got me thinking about starting my own little business. You know, like they sell their homemade pies and breads to stores and restaurants here? I could sell the things I do best —the sweets."

"Really? I wouldn't have guessed you'd have an interest in something like that."

"I didn't," Meg admitted, "until I started baking here every day. I used to do it a lot more when the kids were little, remember? I forgot how much I liked it."

"Wow. I have to admit, this is all news to me. But I guess it makes sense."

She shrugged. "It doesn't matter. It's a ridiculous idea. You need a kitchen with decent equipment, more than one oven. You need money to invest. Most important, you need customers. I'm not going to find any of those things in Homer."

"Hmm. Unfortunately, I see what you mean," he said.

"Worse, what I *am* going to find there are Harlan and Frances. Killers of dreams. Destroyers of spirits."

He picked up the theme. "Experts at extinguishing the fires of hope. Stompers-on of hearts."

They looked at each other and burst out laughing.

When they had quieted down, he looked at her seriously. "Meg, I promise we'll come up with something. I don't know what it'll be, but something."

"There's a promise to hang my hat on," she said.

He smiled. "You mean your bonnet?"

"My bonnet, yeah." Her tone turned wistful. "If only we could just stay here. You think we'd make good Amish farmers?"

He sighed briefly. "No, we wouldn't. We'd make terrible Amish farmers. And we can't stay here."

"I know." She straightened up. "We'd better be getting back."

As she started walking toward the house, she heard his voice behind her.

"I love you, Meg."

She stopped, not turning around. She wasn't sure what to say. In the end, she said nothing but just kept going.

Chapter 16

James's prediction turned out to be correct, and several inches of fresh snow covered the ground by the next day. Everyone gathered around the breakfast table to eat before setting out together for the school's annual Christmas pageant. Meg knew that Rachel and Aaron had been working hard on learning their parts. They were practically bursting with excitement and anticipation, especially since they were rarely allowed to perform in front of people this way.

They all piled into buggies and set out for the small schoolhouse. Leaving their outerwear on the porch, parents filed into the classroom to sit on desks and benches around the room. The Hobarts split up, and Meg and Sam found a spot for themselves in a corner. She was charmed by the children's colorful drawings of farm and winter scenes she saw hung up around the room. She studied the handwritten program, enjoying the whispers and rustling of the children preparing to start.

Meg sat entranced throughout the pageant.

269

The children studied English in school and spoke mostly in English during the program, welcoming their guests, performing religious poems, skits, and songs, all from memory. Their parents smiled and laughed where appropriate, but Meg noticed they did not applaud. Sam had helped Aaron practice his poem and was so thrilled to see his friend get through it flawlessly, he started to clap at the end. When he realized he was the only one doing so, his face turned beet red. Meg put an arm around him. "No big deal," she whispered in his ear. "I'm sure Aaron appreciated that you were glad for him."

Afterward the parents presented the finished quilt to Sarah, the teacher, who accepted it with warm thanks. She, in turn, handed out gifts of a pencil and small notepad to each student.

Back at the house the children were in high spirits. They had lunch, and most of the household took advantage of the snow to go back outside for hours of play. Catherine and David even joined Meg and James for some snowball tossing.

Later, when Jonathan brought a sleigh around front, James, Meg, and Sam hopped in with Aaron and Rachel. As she settled in, Meg spotted a car pull up and park some thirty feet away. Two heavyset strangers, a man and a woman, got out and stood there, staring at the Lutz family. The man began taking pictures of them. Meg watched in annoyance. She believed most tourists were aware that photography was not welcomed by the Amish, although they may not have known the reason was that pictures represented a forbidden graven image. Even if they didn't know, she thought, frowning, what kind of people felt it was all right to park in a family's front yard—*any* family's front yard—and shoot pictures of them?

She wondered how the Amish could bear being gawked at this way. With a guilty start, she recalled that she and her family had originally come here to learn something about these supposedly quaint people.

We were only going to see a film about them, she halfheartedly reassured herself, not park outside their houses as if they were animals in a zoo. Still, she could envision her own family on the road, driving by Catherine and David in their buggy as she or James pointed out to the children the novelty of the clothing and transportation. She was embarrassed by the memory of her own ignorance.

Meg saw the woman tilt her head as if puzzled, then lean toward the man and say something as she pointed in Meg's direction. Meg tapped James, who sat beside her, on the shoulder.

"Look," she said. "Those tourists over there. They're watching the show, the Amish-at-Play. But now they see these crazy English people in the middle of all of them. They're wondering what the heck we're doing here."

James looked over to see. He grinned and gave the people a huge wave. "We're the real Amish," he shouted to them. "The rest of these people are just phonies in costumes. They've kidnapped us. Please help!"

"James!" Meg's reprimand dissolved into laughter.

Her husband laughed, too. They could hear David chuckling up front. The onlookers appeared disgusted before they got in their car and drove away.

Meg and James continued to laugh a few seconds past the point when their amusement wore off—only because they were both enjoying the now-rare sound of their laughter together.

After everyone had come back in for hot chocolate and cookies, Meg and Lizzie found themselves cleaning up alone in the kitchen. Meg washed the dishes while Lizzie filled a small bucket with water and fetched a mop for the floor.

"Why is it," Lizzie asked her mother, wringing out the mop, "that the men and women here have such incredibly stereotypical roles? I mean, talk about so-called women's work and men's work—they've got it covered."

Meg didn't answer immediately. "That's a tough one," she said finally, "because you and I are looking at it from our perspective. We can't really understand their perspective."

"What difference does that make?" Lizzie said, pulling chairs away from the table so she could clean underneath it. "Don't the women ever want to do anything else?"

"Well, wait. Some of them run businesses, right? Like restaurants and stores. The women in this house have a business with the food they sell. You're just looking at the housework part."

"Okay, I'll give you that."

"When you think about it, didn't we have a traditional arrangement in our house? Dad went to the office and I ran the house."

"Yeah, but this seems way more intense."

"I think it's more complicated than that. But I guess I prefer to admire how many skills the women have. Also, they have this calm approach to whatever they do, you know, this steadiness about things. It's as if they have this special strength in their body and their spirit."

Lizzie mulled this over. "That's a good way to put it." She stood up and stretched out her back. "And they do know how to do a ton of things."

They worked in silence for a few minutes more.

"You know," Lizzie said, "what's cool is that they can make things they need. They know how to work stuff. It's like they do *real* things. I hope when I'm older, I'll be good at doing real things."

Amazed by these words, Meg stared at her daughter, but Lizzie was too engrossed in pushing the mop back and forth across the floor to notice.

Meg hadn't wanted the day to end, knowing that the next day was Christmas—the day thcy would be leaving for good. Later that night, after taking a shower, she put on a robe and sat on the side of the bed, rubbing her wet hair with a towel. Idly, she wondered if she would bother going back to using a hair dryer when they left.

James entered the room. "Ah, you're here."

"Hi. What've you been up to? Did you say good night to the kids?"

"Yes, I just stopped by their rooms. I was downstairs talking to Catherine."

Feeling the chill of the night air in the room, Meg rubbed her hair more briskly. "Oh?"

"We were on the phone outside with Nina."

Meg stopped what she was doing. "Nina? My Nina, with the inn?"

"The very one."

"Whatever for?"

He sat down next to her and removed the towel from her hands. Then he placed one of her hands in his. "Last night, after you and I talked, I discussed some things with Catherine. She talked to Nina, and we figured it out."

"Figured out what?" Meg was hard-pressed to imagine James and the two women conferring.

"First of all, Nina left this morning for Philadelphia to spend Christmas with some relatives. That's where she's from originally. Anyway, she has an old friend there, this really successful guy who owns six or seven restaurants and a few specialty food stores. She took along some of the stuff you'd given her and drove it right to his house for him to taste. The guy really liked it. He wants to place an order for the restaurants, plus some to sell at the food stores. A huge order, Meg. Really huge. "

Meg stared at him in disbelief. "Are you joking?"

He held up one hand as if taking an oath. "I swear I am not joking."

"That's incredible. That can happen just like that?"

He shrugged. "I guess so. Nina knows the guy, he liked what he tried, he ordered a bunch."

"But wait." Meg seemed to deflate. "I can't deliver that order. I have no place to bake or anything else."

"Now comes the best part," James said, smiling. "Catherine and Nina have lived here an awfully long time, and they know everything and everyone. It didn't take them long to come up with an answer to that. Seems there's a little restaurant about twenty miles from here that's only open for breakfast and lunch. It caters to the businesses in the area, but there's no night life there. The man who owns it is willing to rent you the kitchen from five p.m. to three in the morning. You'd get in there at night, do your baking, and be out before they open. It's pretty cheap, because it's found money for him— obviously the kitchen isn't generating any income in the middle of the night. So everybody's happy."

"But James," she protested, "where are we living? How is this possibly going to work?"

He stood up and started pacing. "Look, Meg, we both know going to your parents' house is a move of total desperation. We can't go there. We shouldn't. And now we don't have to." He stopped in front of her. "If we have income from this Philadelphia thing and Nina's orders, and we use whatever we have left in the bank, we can stay in this area. There are some efficiency apartments that we can rent by the month. We'll work like dogs to see if we can build something. By the spring we'll know one way or the other. If we fail, we're no worse off than we are now, right?"

Meg stared at him. "You've really thought this through, haven't you? I can't believe it."

He sat back down beside her. "This is truly the least I could do—to try and help you achieve something that you want."

"But what about the kids?"

"The kids'll be fine. They'll start at a local

school after New Year's, so their days are already set. With your night hours and whatever else—they'll just put up with what they have to put up with." He smiled. "I think they probably would have flipped out if this had come about a few months ago. But they can do it now."

"You feel certain?"

He nodded. "More than that. I talked to them about it just before supper. They're game."

"You're joking! And nobody said anything to me?"

"I asked them not to. I wanted to hear what happened with the Philadelphia guy first."

Meg ran a hand through her damp hair. "I am —I'm dumbstruck." She paused. "What are *you* going to do? This can't work if you have nothing to do."

"Where'd you get the idea that I'd have nothing to do? To begin with, I'll be your business manager. Your job is to bake. I need to do the paperwork, order your supplies, do shipping, handle everything other than making the food. The biggest thing I need to do is get you new clients. Somebody's got to be selling."

"I guess that makes sense . . ." she said slowly.

"And I've come up with a second job to do at the same time."

"Really?"

"You've seen the furniture they make here? One day I was helping Joseph Lutz move some things out of his basement, and I saw he had about half a dozen bureaus down there, these incredible handmade chests of drawers. We got to talking about all the carpentry work the Amish men do to supplement their incomes. Some of them do it at home, and sometimes they work directly for factories."

"You're going to become a carpenter?" Meg sounded exactly as skeptical as she felt.

He laughed. "No, I'm not good enough for that. But hey, we come from North Carolina, the furniture capital of the country, and I know people who can connect me to the right places.

"I want to help with this stuff, to sell it to people who are dying for it even if they don't know it right now. I know the carpenters we've met have some distribution already, but I'm hoping I can expand that." He paused. "I want all of us to maintain our connection to these people. And in a small way it could encourage their financial independence. It could make money for us and for them."

"Wow," Meg breathed. "This is a lot to take in."

"From talking to Joseph and David, I understand now how much work goes into the furniture. It's rare to get something of this quality at such decent prices." James laughed again. "I should know, considering all the overpriced junk I insisted we buy for our house. But I also like the idea of supporting their work. It's kind of the least I can do for the community. They saved us —in more ways than one."

"So I guess you'll have plenty to keep you busy."

"Yes. Although the focus has to be on your new business."

James looked her directly in the eyes. "Please let me help make this happen for you. You deserve it. And I owe it to you. We both know that. Please, Meg, give it a chance."

Meg sat in silence. He had covered every angle and every possible objection. He truly wanted her to allow him to do this for her. When he asked her to give it a chance, he wasn't just talking about the business. For the first time since Thanksgiving she saw genuine remorse in his eyes. She also saw fear that she would say no.

She considered the extraordinary generosity behind the offer. Here was a guy who, until a few months ago, was a powerful executive. Now he was encouraging her to follow her own small dream. And he was willing to give it everything he had to make it work for her. It reminded her of why she had fallen in love with him in the first place.

She looked at him and nodded. Relief flooded his face. He put his arms around her and brought her close. She rested her head against his shoulder, inhaling his familiar smell, feeling his hand stroking her hair. It had been a very long time since they had sat like this.

She couldn't say she was going to forgive and forget all he had done, all he had put them through, but she was willing to try. And up until now that had been something she hadn't even dared to hope she would ever feel again.

Chapter 17

Christmas Day was overcast, the air outside frigid. Gusting wind created swirls of powdered snow lifted from the ground. Inside the house the Lutz and Hobart children were sitting near the fire, listening to Old Samuel reading from the Bible. Lizzie occasionally wandered over to stir the contents of the large pot on the stove, a thick pea soup. Despite their having recently consumed lunch, the soup would remain there, warming all day, for anyone who cared to take a bowl. Lunch had been even more crowded than usual, with nearly thirty adults and children feasting on turkey and ham, German potato salad, carrot-and-raisin salad, green beans, noodles, potatoes, cheese, bread, chocolate cake, and carrot cake.

The sky grew dark enough for Catherine and Meg to set out candles to add to the light of the kerosene lamps. As she moved about the house, Meg kept glancing out the window at the Mustang parked at the far end of the dirt drive. James had driven it back to the farm yesterday.

He had told her the repair shop had done an excellent job. It did indeed look like a new car, every surface polished and gleaming—almost like a crouching animal, she thought, lying in wait.

David explained to Meg and James that the family celebrated Christmas for two days and normally would exchange gifts on the second day. However, since the Hobarts were leaving the following morning, they would share gifts today. When Old Samuel finished his reading, adults and children alike sang a hymn. Then everyone scurried to retrieve the presents they planned to give and reassembled several minutes later, the children bright-eyed with anticipation.

The gifts for the Lutz children were in bags or plain paper wrapping. Rachel received a book and a new dress made by her mother. All the boys got socks. For Amanda, there was a quilt made by Catherine and several china plates to add to her collection for when she got married. Aaron was thrilled to receive a much-begged-for skateboard of his own, and Jonathan got a pair of binoculars for his new hobby of bird-watching. Eli and Benjamin got shovels and trowels. The children had made special cards and ornaments for one another. Meg and James were touched to see they had included Lizzie, Will, and Sam, providing each of them with angels and stars.

Watching Aaron examine his new socks, Meg

remembered the years her parents had given her socks or something equally practical for Christmas. Why had that felt so empty and disappointing when this felt so loving?

"For you," Catherine said, handing a large, flat package to Meg. "From all of us."

Meg pulled away the brown paper to reveal four large cookie sheets.

"To get started," David said. "Proper tools are important."

Meg fought the tears that threatened to fill her eyes. She hugged the pans to her. "I'll think of you with everything I bake. Which I would have done anyway." She smiled. "This is the most wonderful present. I'll treasure them. Thank you."

"And for James," David said, handing him a bag.

James reached in to pull out a can of WD-40, pliers, and a screwdriver.

"You need to keep things running smoothly," David said with a smile. "This will help."

James laughed. "You're right, as usual. Thank you."

Meg had knitted mufflers for David, Catherine, and all their children. Knowing they would not wish to draw undue attention to themselves, Meg had chosen black wool for the adults and dark gray for the rest. Sam had done an excellent job in buying the wool, the assignment she had given him when he made the trip to the store with Leah and Old Samuel. The yarn was so perfect, so sturdy yet soft, that Meg was certain Leah had been the one to make the selection. Meg had made the scarves in her room to keep the gifts secret. All of the recipients seemed genuinely pleased.

She and her family had agreed that they wouldn't exchange gifts among themselves. The children had accepted the news without a word of complaint.

Which was why Meg was so surprised when James handed her a small brown cardboard box tied with a red ribbon. "I know we said we wouldn't," he told her, "but this is different."

Puzzled, Meg untied the ribbon and opened the box. She reached inside to lift out the object within. Her eyes widened as she realized what it was. "Oh my . . ." she breathed. "Did you make this?"

"Joseph helped me," James said. "Okay, he helped me a *lot.*"

Meg turned it around in her hands to look at it from all angles. It was an almost perfect replica of a telephone table, an old-fashioned combination of a wooden chair attached to a table designed to hold a phone, and beneath it, a space for a phone book to rest. Back when Meg and James were still college students, before they started dating, Meg had come upon the full-size version of this telephone table in the street, abandoned by a curb. It wasn't particularly well made or of good wood, but Meg was intrigued by its art deco design and the fact that the need for such an item had long ago passed into oblivion. She dragged it back to her college dorm to keep. Although the bulky piece served little purpose, mostly taking up precious space in her small room, she loved it for its charm and impracticality. The idea of sitting in one spot for no other purpose than talking on the phone, and the idea that telephoning had once been a major activity requiring your full attention—she was taken by the romance of the entire notion.

When she and James married, the telephone table came to their apartment. James thought it was ugly and useless. From the day they moved in, he had asked Meg to get rid of it. She adamantly refused. It was both a reminder of her life as a student and a beloved orphan she had saved from destruction. But eventually, she'd allowed James to shove it into an out-of-the-way spot. When they moved to their first house, he protested that it was an eyesore, and it was relegated to the basement. By the next move, Meg realized the table would never see the light of day again. When James asked if she would please donate it to Goodwill, she gave in, hoping someone else would love it as she had.

Here it was now, a five-inch replica, every

detail exact. James had carved it out of plywood, then sanded and shellacked it until it shone.

"You loved that table. It meant something to you," he said. "I had no right to ask you to get rid of it. Heck, you should have put it dead center in the house if you wanted to. I'm really sorry about that." He smiled. "Along with a lot of other things."

Meg looked at him. "Thank you, James," she said.

The rest of the day passed quickly, with Christmas storytelling and more singing of hymns. Supper was only somewhat lighter than lunch. Meg and James joked about how lucky they were to be getting away from all this fattening food, while the Lutzes teased that the two of them would be too weak to work hard enough to be of any use.

After supper, the older boys went to visit some friends, and the rest of the children spent one last night playing games together. They went to bed earlier than usual, because the Lutz family was leaving at six a.m. to spend the day with relatives who lived a three-hour ride away. When it came time to say good night, the children all exchanged hugs. The Lutz children, Meg noticed, were affectionate and composed. It was clear that they were sorry to see their new friends go, but they remained cheerful. Will, Lizzie, and Sam were more visibly upset, Lizzie and Sam in particular getting teary-eyed over their farewells. James reminded them that they would be living under fifty miles away. The Hobarts would be driving back often to visit.

When the children were settled in for the night, Catherine and Meg sat at the kitchen table to share a final cup of tea. As soon as Meg started to look for the words to express her appreciation, Catherine cut her off. "Please do not say these things." Despite the firmness in her tone, she looked pleased. "Instead, I will tell you something. Benjamin is coming home for good. He told us today."

"Oh, that's wonderful," said Meg, thrilled that it had been brought out in the open in time for her to share the good news with Catherine. "It's beyond wonderful." Meg reached across the table to take the other woman's hand. "I can only guess at what you've been going through. I'm so happy for you."

Catherine smiled at her. "Thank you, my friend."

They drank their tea in an easy silence. When they had finished, Catherine took their cups and washed them out, standing them upside down in the dish drain. She turned to face Meg. "So you are leaving, but we will see you again, yes?"

"Yes."

"You won't forget us?"

Meg smiled. "Not likely."

Catherine nodded. "When you come to visit, you will bring us some brownies. One thing less for me to bake."

"It's a deal."

"And when summer comes, I will show you how we make the jams and preserves like you see downstairs." Catherine grinned. "I think you will find time for it."

Meg laughed, astonished that Catherine remembered her earlier comment about always being too busy to learn. She came around to Meg and gave her a hug. "I believe you will all be fine. This will be a good thing for you."

Meg was startled. It was the first personal comment Catherine had made about the Hobarts' situation.

Catherine looked at Meg with her customary directness. "You will be all right. And you come see us soon." With a nod, she turned and left the room.

In the morning the Hobarts were subdued as they made their final preparations to go. Quietly, they gathered whatever last belongings had migrated around the house and finished packing their small bags.

Meg shivered in the cold morning air as she dressed. Tucking in her shirt, she felt something in one of her pants pockets. She reached in to discover the refrigerator magnet she had taken from the house as she walked out the door in Charlotte.

Esse quam videri. To be, rather than to seem.

She stared at it. The motto had been her inspiration for so long, as she tried to *feel* the way she thought she should be, rather than just to *seem* to feel it. Now she saw it in a completely different way. These people, Catherine and David and even their young children, had shown her what it meant to *be* rather than to *seem*. They didn't talk about what they did, how they felt about it, or what it meant. They knew how to just *be*. They knew what they valued: religion, community, work. They followed those values, and as a result they were completely genuine in everything they did. To be, rather than to seem. A far, far harder ideal than Meg had ever imagined.

When James and Meg went downstairs with their bags for the last time, they found Sam with Old Samuel. Sam was clutching Rufus, tearfully burying his face in the puppy's neck.

"I go to get my wife, and we will leave now, Young Samuel. So we must say goodbye," Old Samuel said.

Tears wetting his face, Sam rushed into the older man's arms. "Goodbye, Old Samuel," he managed to get out.

Samuel patted him on the head and stepped back. Sorrowfully Sam extended Rufus to him. "What is this?" Old Samuel asked.

"We're leaving, too, so could you take him now?"

Samuel shook his head. "Everyone knows this dog belongs to you. He must go with you, wherever you go."

Sam looked stunned. "You want me to take him?"

"The two of you are always together. He is your dog."

"I can't just take him."

"Why not? We have many dogs here. We will have more dogs again. I know you will take good care of Rufus."

Sam looked at his parents.

Meg turned to James. "Will they let us have a dog at this place?"

"I'm not sure." He thought for a moment. "Wait, I think I saw a dog near the front door there. Somebody has one, even if it's just the owner."

"Then it's fine with me," Meg said. "What do you say?"

James looked at Sam. "Congratulations, sport. You are now a dog owner."

Shock and joy lit up Sam's face as he turned back to Old Samuel. "This is the best thing that's ever happened to me. Thank you."

Old Samuel rested his hand on Sam's head once more. "Many more best things will happen to you, Young Samuel." The old man turned to go but paused. He addressed himself to Meg and James. "Take good care of my young friend."

Then the three of them were alone.

"Wait until I tell Lizzie and Will," Sam burst out, rushing toward the stairs.

James brought the Mustang up the roadway, close to the front of the house. This time the children helped pass bags to their parents as they packed the trunk, and all five of the Hobarts walked around the house one last time to make sure nothing was left behind.

No one had to give voice to what they were all thinking: how strange it felt to be getting into a car instead of a horse-drawn buggy. When James slammed the trunk shut, the children took their pillows and blankets into the car and shoved their small extra bags beneath their feet. Sam was still relegated to the least comfortable spot, the middle of the backseat, but now he had Rufus on his lap.

The sun had risen to shine brightly in a crisp blue sky. When they were all settled into the car, James turned the ignition key, and they heard the familiar sound of the engine coming to life. Slowly, they drove the length of the roadway. Every one of them turned for a last look at the big white house, at the barn, at the attachment where Old Samuel and Leah lived, at the houses next door and across the road.

James braked at the end of the dirt road, then made a right turn and picked up speed on the main road. Through the swells and dips of the hills they saw the farms and homes extending in all directions. Here and there they observed gray buggies, singly or in pairs, moving along the snowy roads.

From the backseat, Will's voice was jarring. "Can you believe this place?"

Meg and James turned to look at him, aghast at the all-too-familiar snide tone.

"Kill me now," Lizzie answered.

It took but a moment for everyone to recognize the words. They were what the two had said when they first set eyes on the Lutz farm.

The family's laughter echoed as the car turned onto the highway.

About the Author

CYNTHIA KELLER lives in Connecticut with her husband and two children.

Center Point Publishing
600 Brooks Road ● PO Box 1
Thorndike ME 04986-0001 USA

(207) 568-3717

**US & Canada:
1 800 929-9108**
www.centerpointlargeprint.com